Benya Krik, the Gangster

ISAAC BABEL

Benya Krik, the Gangster and Other Stories

EDITED BY AVRAHM YARMOLINSKY

SCHOCKEN BOOKS • NEW YORK

First SCHOCKEN PAPERBACK edition 1969

Library of Congress Catalog Card No. 70-101637

Printed in the United States of America

Walter Morison's translation of "The King" is reprinted from RUSSIAN HUMOROUS TALES *by permission of Sylvan Press Limited, London. "A Father" was translated by Bernard Guilbert Guerney. The remaining stories were translated by the editor.*

Contents

—

Benya Krik, the Gangster

How It Was Done in Odessa 7
A Father 21
The King 36

A Jewish Boy

The History of My Dovecot 47
In the Basement 65
The Awakening 78

The Revolution

Gedali 89
The Rabbi 94
The Rabbi's Son 98
Karl Yankel 102

About the Author 115

Benya Krik, the Gangster

—

How It Was Done in Odessa

I WAS the one to open the conversation.

"Reb Arye Leyb," I said to the old man, "let us talk about Benya Krik.* Let us talk about his meteoric beginnings and his terrible end. Three black shadows block the paths of my imagination. Here is one-eyed Froim Grach. The rusty steel of his deeds — can you compare it to the dazzling strength of the King? And here is Kolka Pakovsky. This man's simple-minded ferocity had in it all that is needed for domination. And is it possible that Haim Drong couldn't recognize the brilliance of the new star? How is it, then, that Benya Krik alone reached the top of the rope ladder, while all the others were left hanging below on the limp rungs?"

Reb Arye Leyb, sitting on the cemetery wall, kept still. Before us stretched the green peace of the graves. A man who thirsts for knowledge must be patient. A man who possesses knowledge should be

* This character was allegedly modeled on Misha Yaponchik, a notorious Odessa gangster. It is said that at one time he headed the Jewish self-defense organization in Odessa, that he fought with the Reds against the White troops and was executed by a firing squad.—*Ed.*

dignified. That is why Arye Leyb remained silent, perched on the cemetery wall. At last he said:

"Why he, why not they, you want to know. Well, forget for a while that you've got spectacles on your nose and autumn in your soul. Stop raising hell at your desk and stammering in public. Imagine for a moment that you're a fellow who raises hell in public squares and stammers on paper. You're a tiger, a lion, a wildcat. You can spend the night with a Russian woman, and the Russian woman will be satisfied by you. You are twenty-five. If sky and earth had rings fastened to them, you would grab these rings and draw the sky down to the earth. And your papa is Mendel Krik, the teamster. What does such a father think about? He thinks about drinking a good glass vodka, about socking someone on the jaw, about his horses — and about nothing else. You want to live, and he makes you die twenty times a day. What would you have done if you'd been in Benya Krik's boots? You'd have done nothing. But he did something. That's why he's King, while you fig with your fist in your pocket.

"Benya, he went to Froim Grach, who then already looked at the world with one eye and was what he is today. He said to Froim: 'Take me on, Froim. I want to be cast upon your shore. The shore I'm cast upon will gain by it.'

"Grach asked him: 'Who are you? Where are you coming from? And what do you live by?'

" 'Try me, Froim,' answered Benya, 'and let's stop chewing the rag.'

" 'Let's,' said Grach. 'I'll try you!'

"And the gangsters held a session to put their minds to the subject of Benya Krik. I wasn't at that session. But it is said that they did hold it. The late Lyovka Byk was elder then.

" 'What's going on under this Benchik's hat?' asked the late Lyovka Byk.

"One-eyed Grach gave his opinion: 'Benya doesn't talk much, but there's a flavor to his words. He says little, and you wish he'd say more.'

" 'If that's so,' exclaimed the late Lyovka, 'then let's try him on Tartakovsky.'

" 'Let's try him on Tartakovsky,' the council decided, and all those who housed a conscience blushed when they heard this decision. Why did they blush? You'll find out if you go where I'll lead you.

"Among us, Tartakovsky had the nicknames Yid-and-a-Half or Nine Holdups. He was called Yid-and-a-Half, because no one Jew could contain so much insolence and so much money as Tartakovsky. He was taller than the tallest policeman in Odessa and he weighed more than the fattest Jewess. And he was nicknamed Nine Holdups because the firm of Lyovka Byk and Company had held up his place not ten or eight times, but exactly nine. It now fell to Benya's lot to hold up Yid-and-a-Half for the tenth time. When Froim passed this information on to him, Benya said 'Yes' and walked out, slamming the door. Why did he slam the door? You'll find out if you go where I'll lead you.

"Tartakovsky has the soul of a murderer, but he's one of ours. He came from among us. He is our own flesh and blood, as if one mother brought us into the world. Half Odessa was employed in his stores. And it was his own Moldavanka people who made trouble for him. Twice they kidnapped him for ransom, and once during a pogrom they staged his funeral, with a choir too. That was when the thugs from the Sloboda section were beating up the Jews on Bolshaya Arnautskaya Street. Tartakovsky ran away from them and came across a funeral procession with a choir.

" 'Who are they burying with a choir?' he asked.

"The passers-by told him it was Tartakovsky's funeral. The procession reached the Sloboda cemetery. Then our people took a machine-gun out of the coffin and made it hot for the Sloboda thugs. But Yid-and-a-Half hadn't expected that. Yid-and-a-Half was scared to death. And who in his position wouldn't have been scared?

"The tenth holdup of a man who had been buried once already — that was really uncivil. Benya, who wasn't King then yet, understood it better than anyone else. But he had said 'Yes' to Grach, and the same day he wrote Tartakovsky a letter like all letters of that kind:

" 'Highly Esteemed Ruvin Ossipovich!

" 'Be so kind as to place under the rain-water barrel next Saturday . . .' and so on. 'Should you take it upon yourself to refuse, as you have recently done on several occasions, a grave disappointment in your family life awaits you.

Respectfully, one whom you know,
Benzion Krik.'

"Tartakovsky, no dawdler, wrote his answer without delay:

" 'Benya!

" 'If you were an idiot, I would have written to you as to an idiot. But I know that you are not, and God forbid that I should have to change my opinion. It looks as if you're making believe you're a child. Don't you know that there has been a bumper crop in Argentina and that we sit here and don't find one customer for our wheat? And upon my word, I'm tired of eating such bitter bread in my old age and having such a disagreeable time of it, after slaving all my life like the lowest teamster, and what do I have after a lifetime of hard labor? Ulcers, sores, aggravation, sleeplessness. Give up them fool ideas, Benya.

Your friend, much more than you imagine,
Ruvin Tartakovsky.'

"Yid-and-a-Half did his part. He wrote the letter. But the postoffice didn't deliver it. When he got no answer, Benya got mad. The next day he showed up in Tartakovsky's office with four friends. Four masked young men carrying revolvers barged into the room.

" 'Stick 'em up!' they said and began brandishing their guns.

" 'Calm down, Solomon,' Benya remarked to one

who shouted louder than the others, 'don't get into this habit of being nervous when you're on the job,' and turning to the clerk who was white as death and yellow as clay, he asked him: 'Is Yid-and-a-Half at the plant?'

" 'The proprietor is not at the plant,' answered the clerk, whose name was Josif Muginstein and who was the bachelor son of Aunt Pessya, – she sold chickens on Seredinsky Square.

" 'Who is in charge here, then?' they asked the unhappy Muginstein.

" 'I am in charge here,' answered the clerk, as green as green grass.

" 'Then with God's help, open the cashbox for us!' Benya ordered him, and so began an opera in three acts!

"Solomon, the nervous one, packed cash, securities, watches and jewelry into a suitcase; the late Josif stood facing him with lifted hands; in the meantime Benya was telling stories from the life of the Jewish people.

" 'If he makes believe he's a Rothschild,' Benya was saying, referring to Tartakovsky, 'then let him burn on a slow fire. Explain it to me, Muginstein, as to a friend: he gets a business letter from me; why couldn't he get into a trolley for five kopecks then, and ride up to my place and have a glass vodka with the family and a snack, taking potluck? What kept him from having a heart-to-heart talk with me? "Benya," he could have told me, "thus and thus, here is my bank balance, wait a couple of days, let me get my breath, give me a chance to turn around . . ." What would I have answered? Hog don't meet hog, but man meets man. Muginstein, do you get me?'

"'I do,' answered Muginstein and told a lie, because it wasn't at all clear to him why Yid-and-a-Half, a respectable, substantial man, one of the leading citizens, should take a trolley to have a bite with the family of Mendel Krik, the teamster.

"Meanwhile misfortune was prowling around the house like a beggar at dawn. Misfortune burst into the office with a bang. And although this time it took the shape of a Jew by the name of Savka Butzis, it was as drunk as a water carrier.

"'Haw-haw-haw!' shouted the Jew Savka. 'Beg your pardon, Benchik, I'm late,' and he stamped his feet and waved his arms. Then he fired a shot, and the bullet struck Muginstein in the stomach.

"Are words needed here? There was a man, the man is no more. There lived an innocent bachelor, like a bird on a bough, and now he has perished, stupidly. Came a Jew who looked like a sailor and fired a shot, not at some bottle with a surprise in it, but at a living man. Are words needed here?

"'Clear out!' shouted Benya, and was the last to go. But as he was running off, he took time to say to Butzis: 'I swear by my mother's grave, Savka, you'll lie beside him. . . .'

"Now tell me, young gentleman, you who cut

coupons off other people's bonds, what would you have done if you'd been in Benya Krik's boots? You don't know how you would have acted. But he knew what to do. That's why he is King, while we two sit on the wall of the Second Jewish Cemetery and shade our faces from the sun with our palms.

"Aunt Pessya's unfortunate son did not die at once. An hour after he was brought to the hospital Benya appeared there. He summoned the doctor-in-charge and the nurse and, without taking his hands out of the pockets of his cream-colored pants, he said to them: 'I want to see the patient Josif Muginstein get well. Just in case, let me introduce myself: I'm Benzion Krik. Spare no expense. Camphor, air cushions, a private room – you must give him everything. If you don't, remember that no doctor, not even a doctor of philosophy, needs more than six feet of earth. . . .'

"Nevertheless Muginstein died the same night. And it was only then that Yid-and-a-Half let himself be heard all over Odessa.

" 'Where does the police begin,' he bellowed, 'and where does Benya end?'

" 'The police ends where Benya begins,' sensible people answered, but Tartakovsky wouldn't calm down and in the end this is what happened: a red automobile with a music box in it played the first march from the opera *Laugh, Pagliacci* in Seredinsky Square. In broad daylight the automobile raced up to the little house where Aunt Pessya lived.

"The automobile thundered, spat smoke, glittered brassily, spread a stench of gasoline, and played arias on its horn. A man leaped out of it and walked into the kitchen, where little Aunt Pessya was writhing on the earthen floor. Yid-and-a-Half sat on a chair, waving his arms.

" 'You gorilla!' he shouted when he caught sight of the visitor, 'you bandit, you, may the earth spit out your corpse! Nice fashion you've started, killing living men. . . .'

" 'Mosoo Tartakovsky,' Benya Krik said to him in a quiet voice, 'it's the second day now that I been mourning for the deceased as for my own brother. But I know that you don't give a damn for my young tears. And where, Mosoo Tartakovsky, in what strong box did you lock up shame? You had the gall to send the mother of our late Josif a miserable hundred bucks. My brain, let alone my hair, stood on end when I heard the news. . . .'

"Here Benya paused. He had on a chocolate jacket, cream-colored pants and raspberry boots.

" 'Ten grand, in a lump sum,' he roared, 'and a pension for the rest of her life, may she live a hundred and twenty years. If not, then let's leave this room, Mosoo Tartakovsky, and get into my car.'

"There was a row between the two. Yid-and-a-Half and Benya had words. I wasn't there when the argument took place. But those who were remember it. The two agreed on five thousand outright and a monthly payment of fifty roubles.

" 'Aunt Pessya,' Benya said then to the disheveled little woman who lay on the floor, 'if you need my life, you can have it, but everybody makes mistakes, even God. A terrible mistake has been made, Aunt Pessya. But wasn't it a mistake on God's part to settle the Jews in Russia, where they've had to suffer the tortures of hell? Would it be bad if the Jews lived in Switzerland, where they'd be surrounded by first-class lakes, mountain air and nothing but Frenchmen? Everybody makes mistakes, even God. Open your ears to what I'm saying, Aunt Pessya. You have five thousand in hand and fifty roubles a month till you die, may you live a hundred and twenty years. Josif will have a first-class funeral: six horses like six lions, two carriages for the wreaths, the choir from the Brody Synagogue, Minkovsky himself will sing at your late son's funeral.'

"The funeral took place the next morning. About this funeral ask the beggars who hang around the cemeteries. Ask the synagogue beadles about it, the kosher poultry men or the old women from the Second Poorhouse. Odessa never saw such a funeral, and the world will never see another like it. That day policemen put on cotton gloves. The synagogues were wide open, they were decorated with greenery and blazed with electric lights. Black plumes swayed above the heads of the white horses that drew the hearse. Sixty choir boys walked in front of the procession. Boys they were, but they sang with the voices of women. Elders of the synagogue of the kosher poultry dealers led Aunt Pessya, one at either elbow. Behind them marched members of the Society of Jewish Salesmen, then came attorneys-at-law, physicians and trained midwifes. On one side of Aunt Pessya were poultry-women from the Old Market, on the other the milkmaids from the Bugayovka district, wrapped in orange shawls. They stamped their feet like gendarmes on a holiday parade, and their wide hips gave off the odor of the sea and of milk. The employees of Ruvin Tartakovsky brought up the rear. There were a hundred of them, or two hundred, or two thousand. They wore black jackets with silk lapels and new boots that squeaked like suckling pigs in a sack.

"And now I shall speak as the Lord did on Mount Sinai out of the burning bush. Fill your ears with my words. It was with my own eyes that I beheld all I beheld, sitting here on the wall of the Second Jewish Cemetery, alongside of lisping Moiseyka and Shimshon, from the cemetery office. It was I who saw it, I, Arye Leyb, the proud Jew who is neighbor to the dead.

"The hearse drove up to the cemetery chapel. The coffin was placed on the steps. Aunt Pessya trembled like a little bird. The cantor climbed out of his carriage and started the funeral service. Sixty choir boys echoed him. At that moment a red motor car shot out from behind a bend on the road. It played *Laugh, Pagliacci,* and came to a halt. The people were as quiet as the dead. The trees were silent, and the choir boys, and the beggars. Four men climbed out from under the red roof and, walking slowly, carried to the hearse a wreath of roses the like of which was never seen before. And when the service was over, four men placed their steel shoulders under the coffin and, with eyes blazing and chests thrust forward, marched in the ranks of the Society of Jewish Salesmen.

"In front walked Benya Krik, who had not yet been called King by anyone. He was the first to approach the grave. He stepped on the mound of earth and stretched out his arm.

"Kofman, of the burial brotherhood, ran up to him.

" 'What do you want to do, young man?' Kofman asked Benya.

" 'I want to make a speech,' answered Benya Krik.

"And he made a speech. It was heard by all who wanted to hear. It was heard by me, Arye Leyb, and by lisping Moiseyka, who was perched on the wall beside me.

" 'Gentlemen and ladies,' said Benya Krik, 'gentlemen and ladies,' he said, and the sun stood above his head like a sentry with a rifle. 'You have come here to pay your last respects to an honest toiler who perished for two cents. In my own name and in the name of all those who aren't present here, I thank you. Gentlemen and ladies, what did our dear Josif get out of life? A couple trifles. What was his occupation? He counted other people's money. What did he perish for? He perished for the whole working class. There are people already doomed to death, and there are people who haven't begun to live. And it just happened that a bullet that was flying at a doomed breast pierced that of Josif, who did not get anything out of life but a couple trifles. There are people who know how to drink vodka, and there are those who don't know how to drink it, but drink all the same. The result is that the first get pleasure from both joy and grief, while the second suffer for all those who drink vodka without knowing how. That is why, gentlemen and ladies, after we have said a prayer for our poor Josif, I will ask you to accompany to his grave Savely Butzis, unknown to you, but already deceased. . . .'

"After he made this speech, Benya Krik stepped down from the mound. The people, the trees, the cemetery beggars were all silent. Two grave-diggers carried an unpainted coffin to a near-by grave. The cantor, stammering, finished the prayers. Benya threw the first shovelful of earth into Josif's grave and walked over to Savka's. All the lawyers and the ladies with brooches followed him like sheep. He made the cantor chant the complete service over Savka, and the sixty choir boys joined in. Savka had never dreamed of such a service – believe the word of Arye Leyb, an old oldster.

"They say that on that day Yid-and-a-Half decided to retire from business. I wasn't there when he made that decision. But that neither the cantor nor the choir nor the burial brotherhood asked to be paid – that I saw with Arye Leyb's eyes. Arye Leyb is my name. And I could see nothing more, because the people, after walking slowly away from Savka's grave, began to run as from a house on fire. They rushed away in carriages, in carts and on foot. And only the four who had come in the red car drove off in it. The music box played its march; the car shook and was off.

"'A King,' said lisping Moiseyka, looking after the automobile, the same Moiseyka who edges me off the best seat on the wall.

"Now you know everything. You know who was the first to utter the word, 'King!' It was Moiseyka. You know why he didn't apply that name either to one-eyed Grach or to ferocious Kolka. You know everything. But what good does it do you, if you still have spectacles on your nose and autumn in your soul? . . ."

A Father

Froim Grach had at one time been a married man. That was long ago; twenty years had passed since then. His wife had borne a daughter to Froim at the time, and had died in childbirth. They named the girl Bassya. Her maternal grandmother lived in Tulchin, a money-grubbing, purblind, wretched small town. The old woman had no love for her son-in-law. She used to say of him: "Froim is a teamster, and he has raven-black horses, but Froim's soul is blacker than his horses."

The old woman had no love for her son-in-law and took the newborn child to bring up herself. She and the girl lived together for twenty years, and then the old woman died. Thereupon Baska came back to her father. Here is how it all happened:

On Wednesday, the fifth day of the month, Froim Grach had been carting wheat from the elevators of the Dreyfus Company to the port, for the steamer "Caledonia." By evening he had finished work and driven off for home. On turning off from Prohorovskaya Street he met Ivan Pyatirubel, the blacksmith.

"Greetings, Grach," said Ivan Pyatirubel. "Some

woman or other is banging away at the door of your place. . . ."

Grach drove on, and caught sight of a woman of gigantic stature in his courtyard. She had enormous flanks and cheeks the color of red brick.

"Papa dear," said the woman in a deafening bass, "I'm bored as hell already. I been waiting for you all day. Grandma died in Tulchin, you ought to know."

Grach, who was standing up in his dray, stared at his daughter, his eyes popping out.

"Don't be getting in the way of the horses!" he shouted in desperation. "Take the bridle off the shaft horse – what do you want to do, hurt my horses?"

Grach stood up in the cart brandishing his whip. Baska took the shaft horse by the bridle and led the horses off to the stable. She unharnessed them and went to busy herself in the kitchen. The girl hung her father's foot clouts on a line, scrubbed the sooty teakettle with sand, and started warming up a beef stew in a cast-iron pot.

"You've got such filth here, I can't stand it, papa dear," said she, and threw out of the window the musty sheepskins strewn over the floor. "But I'll get rid of that filth," Baska shouted, and set her father's supper on the table.

The old man took a swig of vodka out of an enamel teapot and polished off the beef stew, a beef stew as fragrant as a happy childhood. Then he picked up his whip and went to sit outside his gate. Baska followed him there. She had put on men's half-boots, an orange dress, and a hat adorned with dangling birds; and now she seated herself on a bench. The evening sauntered past the bench, the sunset's glowing eye dropped into the sea beyond Peresyp Suburb, and the sky was red, as red as a red-letter day on a calendar. All the shops had already shut down on Dalnitzkaya Street, and the holdup men were riding by on their way to Gluhaya Street, heading for Ioska Samuelson's bawdyhouse. They rode along in lacquered carriages, as vivid as hummingbirds, in their gay jackets. Their eyes were bulging; each had one foot extended toward the footboard, and each clutched in an outstretched hand of steel a monstrous bouquet wrapped in tissue paper. Their lacquered light carriages moved slowly along; there was but one fare seated in each carriage, and the drivers, erect on their high boxes, wore bowknots, like ushers at a wedding. Old Jewish women in their kerchiefs listlessly followed the flow of this customary procession with their eyes; they were indifferent to everything, the old Jewish women; the sons of the shopkeepers and shipowners were the only ones who envied these kings of the Moldavanka district.

Solomonchik Kaplun, the son of a grocer, and Monya Artillerist, the son of a smuggler, were among those who averted their eyes from other people's splendor. The two of them walked past Baska, swaying like girls who had come to know love; they whispered awhile together and launched into a pantomime, their arms demonstrating how they would hug Baska, if she wanted it. And lo, Baska did want it, right off, inasmuch as she was but a simple girl from Tulchin, from a money-grubbing, purblind, wretched small town. She weighed a hundred and eighty pounds, and then some; she had lived all her life among such small fry as Podolian middlemen, bookpeddlers and petty contractors in the timber business, and had never seen such people as Solomonchik Kaplun. Therefore, on beholding him, she started scraping the ground with her stout feet shod in men's half-boots, and said to her father:

"Papa dear," said she in a thunderous voice, "take a look at that little gent: he's got little feet like a little doll; I could simply hug such little feet to death. . . ."

"Oho, Mr. Grach," an old Jew sitting alongside whispered then, an old Jew by the name of Golubchik, "I see that your little one wants to be put out to grass. . . ."

"This trouble I've got to have on my head yet," Froim answered Golubchik, toyed awhile with his whip, then went home to bed and fell peacefully asleep, because he hadn't believed the old man. He hadn't believed the old man, and he turned out to be wholly mistaken. The one who wasn't mistaken was Golubchik. Golubchik earned a living by matchmaking on our street; of nights he read the Psalms over the well-to-do dead, and about life he knew all there was to know. Froim Grach was the mistaken one. The one who wasn't mistaken was Golubchik.

And, as a matter of fact, from that day on Baska passed all her evenings outside the gate. She sat on the bench and sewed away at her trousseau. Pregnant women sat alongside her; mounds of linen crept over her widespread mighty knees; the pregnant women swelled up with all manner of tidbits, even as the udder of a cow at pasture swells with the rosy milk of spring, and meanwhile their husbands, one by one, would come home from work. The husbands of the shrewish wives wrung out their beards under the faucet, after which they yielded their place to hunchbacked crones. The crones bathed fat infants in troughs; they slapped the glowing buttocks of their grandsons and wrapped them up in their worn skirts.

And thus did Baska from Tulchin behold the life of Moldavanka, our generous mother – a life chockfull of suckling infants, drying rags, and nuptial nights filled with suburban chic and soldierly tirelessness. A desire seized the girl for the same sort of life for herself, but soon she learned that the daughter of one-eyed Grach could not reckon on a decent match. Thereupon she ceased calling her father "papa dear."

"You redheaded thief!" she would yell at him of evenings. "Come eat your supper, you redheaded thief. . . ."

And this went on until Baska had finished sewing

six nightgowns and six pairs of lace-trimmed panties for herself. Having finished sewing on the lace, she started crying in a high voice, not at all like her own, and said through her tears to the imperturbable Grach:

"Every girl," said she to him, "has her own interest in life, and I am the only one who lives like a night watchman looking after someone else's warehouse. Either you'll do something for me, papa dear, or I'll put an end to my life. . . ."

Grach heard his daughter out. The next day he put on his long sailcloth cloak and set out to call on Kaplun, the grocer, on Privoznaya Square.

Hanging over Kaplun's shop was a gold-lettered sign; it was the foremost shop on Privoznaya Square. Within was the smell of many seas and splendid lives we know nothing of. A boy was sprinkling the cool depths of the shop with a watering can as he sang, a song fit only for grownups to sing. Solomonchik, the proprietor's son, stood behind the counter; ranged upon the counter were olives that had come from Greece, olive oil from Marseille, raisins from Lisbon, coffee in the bean, Philippe & Canot sardines and Cayenne pepper. Kaplun was sunning himself on a glass-enclosed porch, as he put away a watermelon, a red watermelon with black seeds, almond-shaped like the eyes of sly Chinese women. Kaplun's belly was resting on a table in the sun — and the sun couldn't do a thing with it. But just then the grocer caught sight of Grach in his sailcloth cloak and he turned pale.

"Good day, Mosoo Grach," said he, and moved away from the table. "Golubchik warned me you were coming round, and I've got a pound of tea all ready for you, something special, I tell you. . . ."

And he began to talk about this new sort of tea, brought to Odessa on Dutch ships. Grach listened to him patiently, but after a while cut him short, inasmuch as he was only a simple man with no tricks about him.

"I am only a simple man with no tricks about me," said Froim. "I spend my time with my horses, and I stick to my business. I am giving new underwear along with Baska and a couple of old coppers, and I'm there for Baska to look to and if that's not enough for anybody, in a fire he should burn. . . ."

"Why burn?" Kaplun countered hurriedly, and stroked the teamster's hand. "There's no need for such words, Mosoo Grach, because we know you for a man who can help another man, and then too, you can hurt a man, and as for your not being no holy rabbi from Cracow, why, I didn't stand under the wedding canopy with no niece of Moses Montefiore neither, but . . . but we've got a Madam Kaplun on our hands, a very grand lady, and the Lord God Himself couldn't get to know what she wants. . . ."

"Well, I know," Grach, dreadfully calm, cut the grocer short. "I know that Solomonchik wants Baska, but that Madam Kaplun don't want me. . . ."

"Yes, I want you," Madam Kaplun, who had been eavesdropping at the door, shouted at this point, and she came into the sun parlor, all ablaze, with bosom heaving. "I want you, Grach, like a man wants death, I want you like a bride wants boils on her head. Don't you forget that our grandfather, *olav hasholom,* was by groceries, my papa dear, *olav hasholom,* was by groceries, and that we should stick to our line. . . ."

"So stick to your line," Grach answered the blazing Madam Kaplun and went on home.

There Baska was waiting for him, all dressed up in her orange dress, but the old man, without so much as a look at her, spread a sheepskin coat under a cart, lay down, and slept until such time as Baska's mighty arm thrust him out from under the cart.

"You redheaded thief," said the girl in a whisper that did not sound at all like her usual whisper, "why do I have to stand for your trucker's manners, and why are you keeping as quiet as a tree stump, you redheaded thief?"

"Baska," Grach spoke with a dreadful calm, "Solomonchik wants you, but Madam Kaplun, she don't want me. What they're looking for there is a grocer."

And, straightening out the sheepskin coat, the old man crawled in under his cart again, while Baska vanished from the courtyard.

All this happened on a Sabbath, a day of rest. The sunset's purple eye, searching the earth, stumbled upon Grach that evening, snoring under his dray. The impetuous ray flamed reproach at the sleeper and led him out onto Dalnitzkaya Street, which sent forth dust and glitter like green rye in the wind. Tartars were walking up Dalnitzkaya Street – Tartars and Turks with their mullahs. They were returning from their pilgrimage to Mecca, returning home to their Orenburg steppes and to the Transcaucasia. A steamer had carried them to Odessa, and they were on their way from the port to the inn of Lyubka Schneeweiss, nicknamed Lyubka the Cossack. Striped, stiff robes rigidly encased the Tartars who flooded the pavement with the bronze sweat of the desert. White towels were wound about their fezzes, denoting men who had bowed before the dust of the Prophet. The pilgrims reached the corner; they turned toward Lyubka's yard, but could not pass through, because a crowd had collected at the gate. Lyubka Schneeweiss, a huge purse hanging at her side, was beating up a drunken peasant and shoving him toward the middle of the street. With one hand clenched into a fist she was pounding his face as if it were a tambourine, while with the other she held him up to keep him from slumping. Little streams of blood trickled from the peasant's mouth and ears. At first he was pensive and eyed Lyubka as if she were an utter stranger, then he fell on the cobbles and went to sleep, whereupon Lyubka gave him a shove with her foot and went back to her place. Yevzel, the veteran who worked for her as watchman, shut the gate behind her and waved his hand to Froim Grach, who was passing by.

"Greetings, Grach," said he. "If there's anything in the world you want to see, just drop in at our place – you'll find something to laugh at. . . ."

And the watchman led Grach toward the wall near which the pilgrims who had arrived the evening before were sitting. An old Turk in a green turban, an old Turk, green and light as a leaf, was lying on the grass. He was beaded with pearls of sweat, breathed with difficulty, and kept rolling his eyes.

"There," said Yevzel, and straightened the medal on his threadbare jacket, "there is a drama from life for you – out of the opera, *The Sick Turk.* He's about to kick the bucket, the little old man, but you mustn't call a doctor for him, because he who kicks the bucket on his way home from the god Mohammed, is, they think, the luckiest and richest of men – Halvash," Yevzel shouted to the dying man, and went off into peals of laughter, "here comes the doctor to treat you. . . ."

The Turk gave the watchman a look of childlike fear and hatred and turned his head away. Thereupon Yevzel, satisfied with himself, led Grach to the opposite side of the yard, to the cellar where the wineshop was. In the wineshop lamps were already lit and music was playing. Old Jews with dirty beards were playing Rumanian and Jewish airs. Mendel Krik was at a table, drinking wine out of a green glass and telling how his own sons had maimed him – Benya, the elder son, and Lyovka, the younger. He was bawling out his story in a hoarse and frightful voice, exposing his worn-down teeth and letting everybody feel the wounds on his belly. Zaddiks from Volhynia with porcelain faces were standing behind his chair and listening in a trance to the unheard-of boasting of Mendel Krik. They were astonished at everything they heard, and Grach despised them for it.

"The old windbag," he muttered his opinion of Mendel, and ordered wine for himself.

Then Froim called out to the proprietress, Lyubka the Cossack, to come over to him. She was standing near the doorway swearing foully and drinking vodka.

"Talk!" she yelled at Froim, and crossed her eyes in her fury.

"Madam Lyubka," Froim said, and made her sit down beside him, "you are a smart woman, and I have come to you like to my own mother. I am depending on you, Madam Lyubka – first on God, then on you. . . ."

"Talk!" yelled Lyubka and after making a dash across the cellar, came back to her place.

And Grach said:

"The German colonists are having a bumper wheat crop, and in Constantinople groceries are going for a song. You pay three roubles a pood* for black olives but here they bring thirty kopecks a pound. . . .

* One pood equals thirty-six pounds.

The grocers are having it good now, Madam Lyubka, the grocers are raking it in, and if a man was to handle them right, why, a man could strike it rich. But I've been left all alone in my work; the late Lyova Byk is dead now, I can't turn anywhere to find help, and so I'm all alone – as alone as God in heaven. . . ."

"Benya Krik," said Lyubka then. "Benya Krik . . . You tried him on Tartakovsky; what is wrong with Benya Krik?"

"Benya Krik?" Grach repeated, filled with amazement. "And he's single, no?"

"He's single," said Lyubka. "Get him and Baska hitched, give him money, make him a somebody."

"Benya Krik," the old man repeated like an echo, like a distant echo. "I never thought of him. . . ."

He stood up, muttering and stammering; Lyubka dashed ahead and Froim hobbled in her wake. They stepped out into the yard and went up to the second floor, to the quarters of the women whom Lyubka kept for her guests.

"Our bridegroom is with Katyusha," Lyubka told Grach. "Wait for me in the hall," and she made her way into the room at the other end, where Benya Krik was lying with a woman by the name of Katyusha.

"Enough slobbering," said the proprietress to the young man. "First you've got to get yourself fixed, Benchik, and after that you can go ahead and slobber. Froim Grach is looking for you. He's looking for a man to do a job and can't find anybody. . . ."

And she told him everything she knew about Baska and the affairs of the one-eyed Grach.

"I'll think it over," Benya answered her, covering Katyusha's bare legs with a sheet. "I'll think it over; tell the old man he should wait for me. . . ."

"Wait for him," Lyubka told Grach, who had remained in the hallway. "Wait for him; he'll think it over."

The proprietress moved up a chair for Froim, and he sank into an inordinate spell of waiting. He waited patiently, like a peasant cooling his heels in some government office. Behind the wall Katyusha was alternately groaning and going off into peals of laughter. The old man dozed for two hours near Katyusha's locked door, two hours and maybe even more. Evening had long since turned to night, the sky had gone black, and the Milky Way had known its measure of gold, glitter and coolness. Lyubka's wineshop was closed by now, the drunks were strewn over the yard like broken furniture, and the old mullah in the green turban had died toward midnight. Later music had come from the sea, trumpets and French horns from British ships; the music had come from the sea and had ceased, but Katyusha, the thoroughgoing Katyusha, was still stoking her gaudy, her ruddy Russian paradise for Benya Krik. She moaned on the other side of the wall and went off into peals of laughter; old Froim sat on at her door without stirring; he waited until one in the morning and then knocked.

"Man," said he, "are you making fun of me, maybe?"

Thereupon, at long last, Benya opened the door of Katyusha's room.

"Mosoo Grach," said he, abashed, and all aglow, covering his nakedness with a sheet, "when we're young we think that women are the goods; but after all they're no more than straw that is set on fire by nothing at all. . . ."

And, having dressed, he tidied Katyusha's bed, fluffed up her pillows, and went out into the street with the old man. Strolling along, they came to the Russian cemetery and there, beside the cemetery, Benya Krik and one-eyed Grach, the celebrated holdup man, came to an understanding. They agreed that Baska would bring her future husband three thousand roubles as dowry, two blooded horses, and a pearl necklace. They also agreed that Kaplun would have to pay two thousand roubles to Benya, Baska's groom. Kaplun was guilty of family pride . . . Kaplun from Privoznaya Square had got rich on Constantinople olives, he had shown no pity on Baska's first love, and therefore Benya Krik decided to take upon himself the matter of collecting two thousand roubles from Kaplun.

"I'll take that upon myself, papa dear," said he to

his prospective father-in-law. "God will help us, and we'll square accounts with all grocers."

This was said at daybreak, when night had already passed . . . and it is at this point that a new story begins, the story of the fall of the house of Kaplun, the tale of its slow ruin, of incendiarism and gunfire in the night. And all this – the fate of the proud Kaplun and the fate of the girl Baska – was decided on the night when her father and her sudden bridegroom strolled past the Russian cemetery. The lads were dragging their girls behind the cemetery enclosures, and resounding kisses floated over the gravestones.

The King

WHEN the wedding ceremony was over, the rabbi sank into an armchair; then, rising and going outside, he viewed the tables arrayed all down the courtyard. There were so many of them that those right at the end even poked out into Hospital Street. Velvet-spread, they wound their way down the yard like so many serpents with variegated patches on their bellies; and they sang full-throatedly, those patches of velvet, orange and red.

The living quarters had been turned into kitchens. A sultry flame beat through the soot-swathed doorways, a flame drunken and puffy-lipped. The faces of the old crones broiled in its smoky rays; old women's tremulous chins and beslobbered bosoms. Sweat with the pinkness of fresh blood, sweat as pink as the slaver of a mad dog, streamed this way and that over those mounds of exorbitant and sweetly pungent flesh. Not counting the washers-up, three cooks were preparing the wedding feast; and supreme over all the cooks and washers-up reigned the octogenarian Reisl, tiny and humpbacked, as patina'd with tradition as a scroll of the Torah.

Before the feast began, a young man unknown to the guests made his way into the yard. Wanted a word with Benya Krik. Led Benya Krik unobtrusively aside.

"Listen here, King," said the young man. "A word in your ear. I'm from Aunt Hannah in Kostetzkaya Street."

"Right," said Benya Krik, alias the King. "Out with it."

"Aunt Hannah told me to tell you that there's a new police captain down at the station house."

"Knew that much day before yesterday," said Benya Krik. "Go on."

"The captain's gone and gathered the whole lot together and made a speech."

"New brooms," said Benya Krik. "He's planning a raid. Go on."

"Suppose you know, King, when the raid will be."

"It's scheduled for tomorrow."

"For today, King."

"Who said so, boy?"

"Aunt Hannah. You know Aunt Hannah?"

"I do. Go on."

"The captain, I say, assembled all his men and made a speech. We must settle Benya Krik's hash, he said, seeing that where there's an emperor there's no room for a king. Today, when Krik's sister's getting married and they'll all be together, is just the day. We can nab the lot."

"Go on."

"Well, the dicks began to get cold feet. If we raid 'em today, they said, on a day when Krik is celebrating, he'll see red, and then blood will flow. So the captain said, Duty before everything."

"Right. Off you go," said the King.

"What shall I tell Aunt Hannah?"

"Tell her: Benya knows all about the raid."

And so the young man departed. After him went three of Benya's pals. Said they'd be back in half an hour. And so they were. That's all.

Not according to their years did the wedding guests take their seats. Foolish old age is no less pitiable than timorous youth. Nor according to their wealth. Heavy purses are lined with tears.

In the place of honor sat the bride and groom. Today was their day. In the next place sat Sender Eichbaum, father-in-law of the King. Such was his right. One should know the story of Sender Eichbaum, for it is no ordinary story.

How had Benya Krik, gangster and king of gangsters, become Eichbaum's son-in-law? Become son-in-law of a man who owned sixty milch-kine, all save one? The answer lay in a holdup. About a year before, Benya had written Eichbaum a letter.

"Mosoo Eichbaum," he had written, "have the goodness to deposit, tomorrow morning, in the entrance to No. 17, Sofievskaya Street, the sum of twenty thousand roubles. If you fail to comply with this request, something unheard-of will happen to you, and you will be the talk of all Odessa. Yours respectfully, Benya the King."

Three letters, each one more to the point than that preceding, had remained unanswered. Then Benya took steps. They came in the night, nine of them, bearing long poles in their hands. The poles were wrapped about with pitch-dipped tow. Nine flaming stars flared in Eichbaum's cattle-yard. Benya beat the locks from the door of the cowshed and began to lead the cows out one by one. Each was received by a lad with a knife. He would overturn the cow with one blow of the fist and plunge his knife into the vaccine heart. On the blood-flooded ground the torches bloomed like roses of fire. Shots rang out. With these shots Benya scared away the dairymaids who had come hurrying to the cowshed. After him the other bandits began firing in the air. (If you don't fire in the air you may kill someone.) And now, when the sixth cow had fallen, mooing her death-moo, at the feet of the King, into the graveyard in his underclothes galloped Eichbaum, asking:

"What good will this do you, Benya?"

"If I don't have my money, Mosoo Eichbaum, you won't have your cows. It's as simple as that."

"Come indoors, Benya."

And indoors they came to terms. The slaughtered cows were divided fairly between them, and Eichbaum was guaranteed the integrity of his possessions, even receiving a written pledge with affixed seal. But the wonder came later.

During the raid, on that dreadful night when cows bellowed as they were slaughtered and calves slipped and slithered in the blood of their dams, when the torch-flames danced like black maidens and the milkmaids lunged back in horror from the muzzles of amiable Brownings – on that dread night there ran out into the yard, wearing nought save her low-cut shift, Tzilya, the daughter of old man Eichbaum. And the victory of the King was turned to defeat.

Two days later, without warning, Benya returned to Eichbaum all the money he had taken from him; and then one evening he paid the old man a social call. He wore an orange suit; beneath his cuff gleamed a bracelet set with diamonds; he walked into the room, bowed politely, and asked Eichbaum for his daughter's hand. The old man had a slight stroke, but recovered. He was good for another twenty years.

"Listen, Eichbaum," said the King. "When you die I will bury you in the First Jewish Cemetery, right by the entrance. I will raise you, Eichbaum, a monument of pink marble. I will make you an Elder of the Brody Synagogue. I will give up my own business and enter yours as a partner. Two hundred cows we will have, Eichbaum. I will kill all the other dairy farmers. No thief shall walk the street you live in. I will build you a villa where the tramline ends. Remember, Eichbaum, you were no rabbi in your young days. People have forged wills, but why talk about it? And the King shall be your son-in-law; no snotnose, but the King."

And Benya Krik had his way; for he was passionate, and passion rules the universe. The newlyweds spent three months on the fat lands of Bessarabia, three months flooded with grapes, rich food and the sweat of love's encounters. Then Benya returned to Odessa to marry off his sister Deborah, a virgin of forty summers who suffered from goiter. And now, having told the story of Sender Eichbaum, let us return to the marriage of Deborah Krik, sister of the King.

At the wedding feast they served up turkey, roast chicken, goose, stuffed fish, fish-soup in which lakes of lemon gleamed nacrously. Over the heads of defunct geese, flowers swayed like luxuriant plumages. But does the foamy surge of the Odessa sea cast roast chicken on the shore?

All that is noblest in our smuggled goods, everything for which the land is famed from end to end, did, on that starry, that deep-blue night, its entrancing and disruptive work. Wines not from these parts warmed stomachs, made legs ache sweetly, bemused brains, evoked belches that rang out sonorous as trumpets summoning to battle. The negro cook from the "Plutarch," that had put in three days before from Port Said, bore unseen through the customs barrier fat-bellied jars of Jamaica rum, oily Madeira, cigars from the plantations of Pierpont Morgan and oranges from the environs of Jerusalem. This is what the foaming surge of the Odessa sea bears to the shore; this is what sometimes comes the way of

Odessa beggars at Jewish weddings. Jamaica rum came their way at the wedding of Deborah Krik; and so, having gulped their fill like unclean swine, the Jewish beggars began to beat the ground deafeningly with their crutches. Eichbaum, his waistcoat unbuttoned, scanned with puckered eyes the tumultuous gathering, hiccoughing lovingly the while. The orchestra played a fanfare. It was just like a divisional parade: a fanfare – nothing but. The gangsters, sitting in compact rows, were at first excessively embarrassed by the presence of outsiders; later they loosened up. Lyova Katzap cracked a bottle of vodka on the head of his beloved; Monya the Gunner fired a shot in the air. The rejoicings reached their pitch when, in accordance with the custom of older times, the guests began bestowing their wedding presents. *Shammesim* leaped on a table and there, to the stormy wailing of the fanfare, sang out how many roubles had been presented, how many silver spoons. And now the friends of the King showed what blue blood meant, and the chivalry, not yet extinct, of the Moldavanka district. On the silver trays, with ineffably nonchalant movements of the hand, they cast gold coins, rings and threaded coral.

Aristocrats of the Moldavanka, they were tightly encased in raspberry waistcoats; russet jackets clasped their shoulders, and on their fleshy feet the azure leather cracked. Rising to their full height and thrusting out their bellies, the bandits clapped in time with the music; with the traditional cry of "Bitter, bitter!" called on the married couple to kiss, and showered the bride with blossoms; and she, Deborah of forty summers, sister of Benya Krik, disfigured by her illness, with her swollen crop and her eyes bulging from their orbits, sat on a pile of cushions side by side with the feeble youth, now mute with misery, whom Eichbaum's money had purchased.

The bestowal of gifts was drawing to a close, the *shammesim* were growing hoarse and croaky, and the double bass was at cross purposes with the fiddle. Over the courtyard there suddenly spread a faint smell of burning.

"Benya," said Papa Krik, famed among his fellow truck drivers as a bully, "Benya, d'you know what I think? I think our chimbley's on fire."

"Papa," said Benya to his inebriated parent, "eat and drink, and don't let such trifles bother you."

And Papa Krik followed the filial advice. Drink and eat he did. But the smoke-cloud grew more and more pungent. Here and there the edges of the sky were turning pink, and now there shot up, narrow as a swordblade, a tongue of flame. The guests, half rising from their seats, began to sniff the air, and the womenfolk gave little squeaks of fear. The gangsters eyed one another. And only Benya Krik, aware of nothing, was disconsolate.

"The celebration's going all to pieces," he cried, filled with despair. "Good friends, I beg you, eat and drink!"

But now there appeared in the courtyard the same young man as had come earlier in the evening.

"King," he said, "I'd like a word in your ear."

"Out with it, then," said the King. "I've always a spare ear for a spare word."

"King," said the unknown young man, and giggled. "It's really comical: the police station's burning like a candle!"

The shopkeepers were silent. The gangsters grinned. The sexagenarian Manka, ancestress of the suburban bandits, placed two fingers in her mouth and whistled so piercingly that her neighbors jerked away in fright.

"You're not on the job, Manka," observed Benya. "More sang-frwa!"

The young man who had brought these astounding tidings was still doubled up with laughter. He was giggling like a schoolgirl.

"They came out of the station, forty of them," he related, vigorously moving his jaws, "all set for the raid; and they hadn't gone fifty yards when the whole place was on fire. Why don't you folks drop round and watch it burn?"

But Benya forbade his guests to go and view the conflagration. He set out himself with two comrades. The station was in a proper blaze. Policemen, their buttocks waggling, were rushing up smoky staircases and hurling boxes out of windows; the prisoners, unguarded, were running off. The firemen were filled with zeal, but no water flowed when the nearest tap was turned. The police captain – the broom that was to have swept clean – was standing on the opposite pavement; the ends of his moustache curled into his mouth, and he was biting them. Motionless the new broom stood there.

As he passed the captain, Benya gave him a military salute.

"Good health, Your Excellency," he said, deeply sympathetic. "What do you say to this stroke of bad luck? It's a nightmare!"

He stared hard at the burning edifice and slowly shook his head.

"Ai-ai-ai!" he went.

When Benya got back home the little lamps in the courtyard were flickering out and dawn was beginning to touch the sky. The guests had departed and the musicians were dozing, leaning their heads on their double basses. Deborah alone was not thinking of sleep. With both hands she was urging her fainthearted husband towards the door of their nuptial chamber, glaring at him carnivorously, like a cat that, holding a mouse in her jaws, tests it lightly with her teeth.

A Jewish Boy

—

The History of My Dovecot

For Maxim Gorky

As a child, I very much wanted to have a dovecot. In my whole life I never wanted anything more. I was nine when Father promised to give me money to buy the lumber and three pairs of pigeons. This was in 1904. I was studying for the *gymnasia* entrance examination. We were then living in Nikolaev, in the province of Kherson. This province exists no longer, our city now being part of the Odessa Region.

I was only nine and I was afraid of the examination. Even now, after twenty years, it is very hard to make clear how it terrified me. In both subjects – Russian and arithmetic – I had to get no less than an A. The quota in our school was very small; only five per cent. Of the forty boys that were to be admitted to the first year, only two could be Jews. The examiners made it very tough for the Jewish boys; they did not try their tricks on anybody else. That is why Father, when he promised to buy me the pigeons, laid down the condition that I should get two A-plusses. He succeeded in half killing me, and

I sank into an endless nightmare, a child's long dream of despair, and in that trance I went to the examination, and in spite of it all, came out ahead of all the others.

I knew the answers. The teachers, with all their tricks, could not take away my intelligence and my avid memory. I knew the answers, and I received two A's. But that did not help me. Hariton Efrussi, a merchant who exported wheat to Marseille, paid a bribe of five hundred roubles for his son, so they turned one of my A's into an A-minus, and admitted little Efrussi instead of me. My father was heart-broken. Ever since I had been six he had had me taught the necessary subjects, and the incident of the "minus" drove him frantic. He wanted to beat up Efrussi or to get a couple of longshoremen to beat him up, but Mother dissuaded him from such wickedness, and I started cramming for another examination to be taken the following year. Behind my back my parents arranged with my tutor that we should cover the work of both first and second year in one, and as we were desperate by now, I learned three books by heart: Smirnovsky's grammar, Yevtushevsky's arithmetic and Putzykovich's Russian history. These textbooks are no longer used, but I learned them by heart from cover to cover, and the following year, the examiner Karavayev gave me the unbelievable A-plus in Russian language. For a long time my extraordinary triumph was the talk of our town, and my father was so proud of it that I could not bear to think of his petty, insecure existence and of how impotently he submitted to all vicissitudes, merely rejoicing over them or being hurt by them.

I thought more highly of Karavayev. A former Moscow student, he was an apple-cheeked man constantly boiling with indignation. He was hardly thirty years old, and his virile face was as ruddy as that of a peasant lad not yet worn out by hard work, but one cheek was disfigured by a wart which sprouted a tuft of ash-gray hair, like a cat's whiskers. The other examiner was assistant supervisor Pyatnitzky, who was held to be a person of importance in the school and in the entire province. He questioned me about Peter the Great, and forthwith I felt as though I were plunging into oblivion, as though doom were approaching and an abyss opening before me, a parched abyss lined with ecstasy and despair.

About Peter the Great, I knew by heart the passages in Putzykovich's book and in Pushkin's poems. I started reciting the stanzas with a catch in my voice, and suddenly human faces of various colors filled my eyes, like cards from a new pack, all mixed up. While they were being shuffled in the depths of my eyes, I shouted Pushkin's lines at the top of my voice, quivering, rushing, stiffening my back. I kept shouting them for a long time, and no one interrupted my insane screaming, gulping and mumbling. Blinded, possessed by a fierce freedom, I saw nothing but Pyatnitzky's face framed in a silvery beard and bent over the table. He did not interrupt me, but merely whispered to Karavayev who was exulting in me and in Pushkin:

"What a nation these little Yids of yours are—there's a devil in them."

When I stopped, the old man said:

"Good, you can go, my little friend."

I walked out of the classroom into the hall and there, leaning against the unpainted wall, I began to emerge from my anguished trance. Russian boys were playing about me, the school bell hung there over the staircase, and a little watchman was dozing on a chair with a bashed-in seat. I stared at the watchman and began to come to my senses. The children were edging up to me from all sides. They wanted to give me a fillip or just play with me, but suddenly Pyatnitzky appeared in the hall. Walking past me, he halted for an instant, and a slow uneasy wave crept up the back of his coat. I sensed agitation in this broad, fleshy, aristocratic back, and I moved closer to the old man.

"Children," he said, "leave this boy alone," and he laid his plump, gentle hand on my shoulder.

"My little friend," Pyatnitzky continued, turning to me, "tell your father that you have been admitted to the second year."

The splendid star on his breast beamed, the medals on his lapel chimed, and his bulky, black, uniform-clad body began to move away on straight legs.

It was jammed in by the somber walls; it moved between them as a boat moves between the tall banks of a canal, and vanished in the doorway of the director's office. A little servant carried in tea for him with a solemn clatter, and I ran to our store.

A peasant customer was sitting there scratching himself, plagued with indecision. Catching sight of me, Father abandoned the peasant and promptly credited my story. He shouted to the clerk to shut up shop, and was about to rush off to Cathedral Street to buy me a regulation school cap with a badge. My poor mother could hardly tear me away from this crazed man. She was pale, and she peered into the future doubtfully. By turns she fondled me and pushed me away in disgust. She said that the names of those admitted to high school were usually printed in the papers, and that God would punish us and people would jeer at us if we bought the school uniform before it was time. Mother was pale and she peered into my eyes doubtfully, questioning Fate. She looked at me with bitter pity as at a cripple, for she alone knew how unlucky our family was.

All the men of our family trusted people blindly and were given to acting rashly, with the result that we were pursued by ill luck. At one time my grandfather had been rabbi at Belaya Tzerkov, but he was run out of the town for blasphemy. After that he lived on boldly and in dire poverty for forty years, studied foreign languages and in his eightieth year began to lose his faculties. Uncle Lev, my father's brother, attended the Yeshivah of Volozhin; in 1892 he fled the country to avoid military service and carried off with him the daughter of a quartermaster of the Kiev military district. Uncle Lev took this woman to Los Angeles, deserted her there, and died in a bawdyhouse, among Negroes and Malays. After his death the American police sent us his belongings from Los Angeles — a large trunk hooped with brown iron bands. It contained dumbbells, locks of women's hair, grandfather's *tales,* horsewhips with gilt knobs, and jasmin tea in boxes inlaid with false pearls. Of all the men of the family, there remained only my insane Uncle Simon, who lived in Odessa, my father and I. But my father trusted people utterly and implicitly; he offended them by the transports of his affection, they could not forgive him this, and cheated him. For that reason Father believed that his existence was ruled by a malicious Fate, an inexplicable being entirely unlike him, that persecuted him perpetually. And so I was the only man in the family to whom my mother could pin her hopes. Like all Jews, I was undersized and sickly, and I suffered from headaches because of studying too hard. All this was plain to Rachel, my mother, who was never blinded by the beggar's pride of her husband and his baffling belief that some day our ancient line would become grander and mightier than the rest of mankind. She expected nothing of any of us, she did not want to get me the uniform and consented only to having a large photograph taken of me. Nevertheless we did have to buy a regulation cap with a badge.

On September 20, 1905, the list of those admitted to the second year was posted at school. My name was on the list too. All our relatives came to stare at this paper, and even Shoyl, my great-uncle – everybody called him grandfather – came to the school. I liked this boastful old man because he sold fish in the market. His fat hands were always damp, covered with fish scales and reeking with the odors of beautiful, chilly worlds. This set Shoyl apart from ordinary people, as did also the tall tales he used to tell about the Polish uprising of 1861. In the old days Shoyl had been innkeeper at Skvira and had witnessed the execution of Count Godlewski and other Polish insurgents by the firing squads of Nicholas I. Maybe he hadn't actually witnessed it. I know now that Shoyl was only an old ignoramus and naïve liar, but I have not forgotten his stories; they were good. And so even this foolish Shoyl came to the school to read the list with my name on it, and in the evening, sure of himself and indifferent to the fact that no one in the world cared for him, he danced and stamped his feet at our beggars' ball.

Father gave the party to celebrate the event and invited his friends – grain merchants, real-estate brokers and commercial travelers who sold agricultural machinery in our part of the country. They sold machinery to anybody. Both peasants and landowners were afraid of them, for it was impossible to get rid of them without making a purchase. Of all the Jews, drummers are the jolliest and most worldly-wise people. At our party they sang Hasidic songs consisting of three words only, but repeated over and over, with a great many droll intonations. Only he can appreciate the peculiar charm of these intonations who has celebrated a Passover with Hasids or who has been in Volhynia in their noisy synagogues.

Besides the traveling salesmen the company included old Lieberman who taught me the Hebrew language and the Torah. We called him Monsieur Lieberman. He drank more Bessarabian wine than he could well carry, the silken *tzitzis* peeped out from under his red vest, and he proposed a toast to me in Hebrew. In his speech the old man congratulated my parents, and said that at the examination I had triumphed over all my enemies, over the Russian boys with fat cheeks and the sons of our coarse money-bags. Thus he declared, in the days of old, David, the King of Judea, had vanquished Goliath, and even as I had triumphed over Goliath, so our unyielding people by the power of its intelligence would vanquish the enemies that surround us and thirst for our blood. Having spoken thus, Monsieur Lieberman broke into tears and weeping drank more wine and shouted "Vivat!" The men formed a circle, pressed him into it and began to dance an old-fashioned quadrille such as they dance at weddings in small Jewish towns. Everybody had a good time at our party, even Mother got tipsy, although she did not like vodka, and did not see how people could like it; for that reason, she regarded all Russians as madmen and did not understand how women could live with Russian husbands.

But our happy days came later. They came for my mother when she was beginning to get used to making sandwiches for me to take to school, or when she was shopping for my school supplies: a pen-and-pencil case, a penny bank, a school knapsack, new books in stiff bindings and notebooks with glossy covers. No one in the world feels the fascination of new things more strongly than do children. A child thrills to their smell like a dog on a hare's trail, and knows an ecstasy which, when we grow up, is called inspiration. And this pure, childish delight in owning things that had the aroma of tender dampness and freshness peculiar to new things was communicated to my mother. It took us a month to get used to the pen-and-pencil case and to the unforgettable morning twilight when I would have tea on the edge of a large lamp-lit table and gather my books into my school knapsack; it took us a month to get used to our happy life, and only after the first half-term did I remember about the pigeons.

I had everything ready for them — one rouble fifty and a dovecot that Grandfather Shoyl had made out of a box. The dovecot was painted brown. It had nests for twelve pairs of pigeons, carved ledges on the roof, and a special grating of my own invention to help me decoy strange birds. Everything was ready. On Sunday, October 20, I was about to set out for Okhotnitzky Square, but a sudden calamity barred my way.

My admission to the second year of high school, of which this is the story, occurred in the autumn of the year 1905. Czar Nicholas was then granting a constitution to the Russian people, and orators in shabby overcoats climbed up on the low pillars near the city hall and made speeches. There was shooting on the streets at night and Mother wouldn't hear of my going to Okhotnitzky Square. Early in the morning of October 20, our neighbors' boys were flying kites right opposite the police station, and our water carrier had knocked off work and was promenading up and down the street, his hair greased and his face red. Then we saw the sons of Kalistov, the baker, drag out a leather-upholstered horse, and start doing gymnastics in the middle of the street. No one interfered with them; in fact Semernikov, the policeman, egged them on to jump higher. Semernikov was wearing a silk belt and his boots had a higher polish than they had ever known. It was this policeman in plain clothes who frightened my mother most of all. That was the reason why she was reluctant to let me go, but I made my way to the street through the back yard, and ran to Okhotnitzky Square, which was far beyond the railway station.

Ivan Nikodimich, pigeon seller, sat in his usual place on the square. In addition to pigeons, he had rabbits for sale and a peacock. The peacock, its dazzling tail spread out, sat on a perch and moved its dispassionate, exquisite little head from side to side. A twisted cord was attached to one of its legs, and the end of it was held down by Ivan Nikodimich's rush chair.

As soon as I got there I bought from the old man a pair of reddish-blue pigeons with sumptuous ragged tails, and a pair of crowned pigeons, and tucked them away in a bag in my bosom. I still had forty kopecks left, but the old man would not let me have a pair of pigeons of the Krukov breed at that price. I loved the short, granular, friendly bills of the Krukov pigeons. Forty kopecks was a fair price, but the trader held out for more and averted from me his sallow face consumed by the solitary passions of the bird-catcher. After considerable bargaining, seeing that there were no other buyers, Ivan Nikodimich gave in. I had my way, and yet it all turned out badly.

At noon or a little later a man in felt boots crossed the square. He walked lightly on swollen legs and his animated eyes were blazing in his wasted face.

"Ivan Nikodimich," he said as he passed by the bird-catcher, "pack up your things; over in the city the Jerusalem gentry are being given the constitution. On the fish market Grandfather Babel has been done in. . . ."

Having spoken, he strode on lightly among the bird cages, like a barefoot plowman walking along the edge of a field.

"Bad business," muttered Ivan Nikodimich after him; "bad business," he shouted more severely, and began to gather up the rabbits and the peacock and shoved the Krukov pigeons at me, accepting forty kopecks. I tucked them away in my bosom and watched the people running from the market place. The last one to leave was the peacock perched on Ivan Nikodimich's shoulder. He sat there like the sun in the moist autumnal sky; he sat as July sits on the pink river bank, red-hot July in the long, cool grass. With my eyes I followed the old man, his cobbler's chair and the darling cages, wrapped up in gay rags. The market place was by now deserted, and the shooting sounded close by.

Then I ran toward the railway station, crossed the square that suddenly fell away from me, and flew into a deserted side street covered with yellow trampled earth. At the far end of the street sat legless Makarenko in his wheel chair; he used to wheel himself around town in this chair and sell cigarettes from a tray. Boys in our street bought cigarettes from him, the children liked him. I made straight for him when I ran into the side street.

"Makarenko," I said, breathless with running, and I patted the cripple's shoulder. "Have you seen my grandfather Shoyl?"

The cripple made no answer. His coarse face, a thing of red fat that spoke of fists and iron, was translucent. He was fidgeting in his wheel chair in great excitement, and his wife, Katyusha, her cotton-padded rump turned to us, was sorting out objects that lay on the ground.

"What have you counted?" asked the cripple, and shrank away from the woman, as though he knew beforehand that her answer would be unbearable.

"Gaiters, fourteen," said Katyusha, without straightening up, "quilt-covers, six; now I am counting the mobcaps."

"Mobcaps!" shouted Makarenko, choked and made a sound like a sob. "Looks like God has elected me, Katerina, to be the scapegoat. People are carrying away whole bolts of linen, everybody else gets his cut, and we get mobcaps."

And indeed, a woman came running along the lane, a beauty, her face aflame. She was carrying several Turkish fezzes under one arm and a bolt of cloth under the other. In a blissful, frantic voice, she was calling to her children who had strayed off; a silk dress and a pale-blue blouse floated in the air, like appendages of her flying form, and she paid no attention to Makarenko who followed her in his wheel chair. The cripple lagged behind her, the wheels rattled, he kept working the levers feverishly, but could not keep up with her.

"Missus," he screamed at the top of his voice, "for God's sake, Missus, where did you get that calico?"

But the woman with the floating dress was gone. A rickety old wagon came round the corner from the opposite direction. A peasant lad was standing in it.

"Where's everybody?" asked the lad and lifted a

red rein above the jades who were leaping in their collars.

"Everybody's on Cathedral Street," said Makarenko imploringly, "everybody's there, my good fellow; whatever you pick up – bring it all here, I'll buy everything."

Hearing the name of the street, the lad wasted no time. He bent over the front of the wagon and whipped up his piebald jades. The horses, like calves, heaved their filthy hindquarters, and broke into a gallop. The yellow lane was again deserted; then the legless man turned his quenched eyes on me.

"Is it that God has elected me?" he said apathetically. "Am I then the son of man?" And Makarenko stretched out toward me a paralytic's hand stained with leprosy.

"What have you got in that bag?" he asked me, and took the bag that had been warming my heart.

The cripple plunged his heavy hand into the bag and pulled a reddish-blue pigeon out into the light. Its claws turned up, the bird lay in his palm. "Pigeons," said Makarenko and, grinding his wheels, rolled over to me. "Pigeons," he repeated, like an inevitable echo, and hit me on the cheek.

He struck me with full force, his fist clutching the pigeon, and the bird was crushed against my temple. Katyusha's cotton-padded rump spun in my pupils, and I fell to the ground in the new coat which was part of my school uniform.

"Their seed must be destroyed," said Katyusha,

straightening her back over the mobcaps. "I hate their seed and their stinking men. . . ."

She said other things about our seed, but I heard no more. I lay on the ground and the entrails of the crushed bird trickled down my temple. They trickled down my cheeks, wriggling, splashing, blinding me. A tender bluish gut of the pigeon crept down my forehead, and I shut the eye which could still see, so as not to behold the world spread out before me. It was small and terrible. Before my eyes lay a pebble weathered to the semblance of the face of an old woman with a large jaw, also a piece of rope and a bunch of feathers, still breathing. My world was small and terrible. I shut my eyes so as not to see it and I pressed against the earth that lay under me in reassuring muteness. This trampled earth was so utterly unlike our life and the threat of examinations in our life. Somewhere far away disaster was riding across it on a white horse, but the noise of the hoofs was growing fainter, ceased, and finally stillness, the bitter stillness that sometimes strikes down children in distress, suddenly obliterated the dividing line between my trembling body and the immobile earth. My earth smelled of moist bowels, of graves, of flowers. I became aware of its odors and broke into tears that had no terror in them.

Then I walked along a strange street piled with white boxes. I walked alone on a sidewalk swept clean as if it were Sunday, and I cried bitterly, unstintedly, satisfyingly, as I was never to cry again in my whole life. The wires, turned white, hummed overhead, a fidgety little mutt ran in front of me, and in a side street a young peasant with a vest on was smashing a window in Hariton Efrussi's house. He was using a mallet and swinging his whole body with it, and, sighing, he beamed in all directions, smiling a good-natured smile of intoxication, sweat and spiritual vigor. The whole street was filled with the crackling, crunching, singing of the scattering splinters. The peasant was swinging his mallet simply that he might sway his body, sweat, and shout extraordinary words in a strange, non-Russian tongue. He shouted and chanted them and kept tearing open his blue eyes, until a church procession entered the street on its way from the city hall. Old men with dyed beards carried in their hands a portrait of a combed and curled Czar, banners with images of sepulchral saints waved over the procession, and fiery old women surged forward uncontrollably. The peasant in the vest, catching sight of the procession, pressed the mallet to his breast and ran after the banners, and I, having waited till the procession had gone past, made my way home.

It was empty, our house. The white doors were wide open; the grass around the dovecot was trampled. Kuzma alone had not deserted the courtyard. Kuzma, the gatekeeper, sat in the shed on Shoyl's corpse, laying out the body.

"The wind carries you about like a bad chip of wood," said the old man, catching sight of me, "you've been gone a dog's age. . . . The people here have gone and finished off our grandfather."

Kuzma sniffled, turned away and started taking a perch out of a rip in grandfather's trousers. Two perches had been stuck into Grandfather: one into a rip in his trousers, the other into his mouth, and though Grandfather was dead, one perch was still alive and twitching.

"They've done for our grandfather and nobody else," said Kuzma, throwing the perch to the cat; "he cursed the hell out of the lot of them, he sure blasted them, the good man. You ought to get five-kopeck pieces for his eyes."

But at the time, being only ten years old, I did not know what dead people wanted with five-kopeck pieces.

"Kuzma," I said in a whisper, "save us."

And going up to the gatekeeper, I threw my arms around his old stooped back with one shoulder higher than the other, and I caught sight of Grandfather from behind this friendly back. Shoyl lay on the floor, which was strewn with sawdust, his chest crushed, his beard sticking up, his bare feet thrust into coarse shoes. His legs, spread wide apart, were dirty, purple, dead. Kuzma bustled about the corpse, he tied up the jaw and kept looking for something else to do for the deceased. He bustled about as though he had just acquired a new possession, and only quieted down after he had combed out the dead man's beard.

"He cursed the hell out the whole lot," he said with a smile, and eyed the corpse lovingly. "If it had been just Tartars, he'd have chased them off, but then those Russians came up, and their women too. Russians just can't bear to forgive anybody, I know Russians."

The gatekeeper strewed more sawdust around the deceased, removed his carpenter's apron and took me by the hand.

"Let's go to your father," he muttered, squeezing my hand tighter; "your father has been looking for you since morning; let's go, or it'll be the death of him." And I went with Kuzma to the tax inspector's house, where my parents had hidden when they ran away from the pogrom.

In the Basement

As a boy I was given to lying. It was all due to reading. My imagination was always on fire. I read in class, during recess, on the way home, at night — under the dinner table, hidden by the folds of the cloth that reached down to the floor. Reading made me miss all the important doings of this world: playing hookey in order to go down to the waterfront, billiards in the cafés on Greek Street, boating off Langeron. I had no chums. Who would want to have anything to do with a fellow like that?

One day I saw a book about Spinoza in the hands of Mark Borgman, who was at the head of our class. He had just finished it and he simply had to tell the boys around him about the Spanish Inquisition. What he said about it was mere scholarly patter. There was no poetry in Borgman's words. I could not bear it and broke in on him. I told all who would listen to me about old Amsterdam, the darkness of the ghetto, the diamond-cutters who were philosophers. To what I had read in books I added much of my own. I couldn't do without that. My imagination heightened the drama of the situations, made the plots more mysterious, altered the endings. Spinoza's death, that free, lonely death of his, I pictured as a battle. The Sanhedrin urged the dying man to repent, but he was adamant. I even brought Rubens into the picture. I had Rubens standing at the head of the bed, making a death mask.

My schoolmates listened agape to my fantastic tale. It was told with enthusiasm. When the bell rang, the group broke up reluctantly. At the next recess, Borgman came up to me, linked his arm with mine and we strolled together. We were friends. Borgman wasn't one of the unpleasant kind of star pupil. His powerful brain found our high school subjects mere doodles on the margin of a real book. Greedily he looked for this book. Even we, twelve-year-old ninnies, realized that an extraordinary life, the life of a scientist, lay in store for him. He did not prepare his lessons, he merely listened in class. This sober-minded and self-restrained boy grew fond of me because of my gift for distorting everything, even the simplest possible things.

The time for promotion was upon us. My report card was full of barely passing marks. I had such a remarkable imagination that my teachers could not bring themselves to flunk me. Early in the summer Borgman invited me to his family's suburban villa. His father was the director of the Russian Bank for Foreign Trade. He was one of those men who were making Odessa another Marseille or Naples. There was in him the mettle of the Odessa merchant of the old days. He belonged to the race of skeptical and affable *viveurs*. He avoided using Russian, preferring the clipped, rather coarse lingo of Liverpool sea captains. When, in April, the Italian opera arrived in town, Borgman would give a dinner for the company at his house. The bloated banker – the last of the Odessa merchant princes – would have a two-month affair with the buxom prima donna. When she left, she would carry memories that did not burden her conscience, and a necklace chosen with taste but not too expensive.

The old man held the post of Argentine consul and was head of the stock exchange. He was very intelligent. It was to his house that I was invited. My aunt Bobka dinned the news into the ears of all the neighbors. She put herself out to dress me up. I took the tram to Great Fountain, getting off at the sixteenth stop. The villa was situated close to the beach on a reddish cliff. On the slope a flower garden was laid out with fuchsias and thujas trimmed to the shape of balls.

I came of a destitute and freakish family. The appointments of the Borgman villa simply took my breath away. Along the garden walks gleamed white cane chairs, shaded by trees and framed in greenery. The dining table had flowers on it, and the window frames were painted green. In front of the house there was a low wooden colonnade.

In the afternoon the banker came home. After dinner he placed a cane armchair at the very edge of the cliff, facing the restless plain of the sea, raised his white-trousered legs, lit a cigar, and started reading *The Manchester Guardian*. The guests, ladies from the city, played poker on the veranda. On the table a slender samovar with ivory handles was humming.

Fond of cards and sweets, fashionable if untidy, and secretly promiscuous, with scented underwear and wide hips, the ladies fluttered black fans and staked gold pieces. The sun shone upon them through a trellis of wild grapes. Its fiery circle was enormous. The women's black hair was heavy with copper-colored lights. Sunset glints pierced their diamonds; diamonds were clapped on everywhere, in the hollows between their breasts, on their rouged earlobes, on their blue-veined puffy feminine fingers.

Evening came. A bat rustled by. The sea grew blacker as it rolled up against the red hillside. My twelve-year-old breast expanded with joy and the ease of other people's wealth. My friend and I, hand in hand, strolled along a distant tree-shaded alley. Borgman told me that he was going to be an aeronautical engineer. It was rumored, he said, that his father would be sent to London as a representative of the Russian Bank for Foreign Trade, and then he, Mark, would be able to go to school in England.

In our home at Aunt Bobka's, no one talked about things like that. I had nothing with which to repay this steady stream of magnificence. So I told Mark that in our house everything was different, but my grandfather Levi Itzkhok and my uncle had been all over the world and had had a thousand adventures. I described these adventures one after another. Immediately all sense of the possible left me and I took Uncle Wolf through the Russo-Turkish War, then on to Alexandria, to Egypt. . . .

The night stood erect among the poplars, the stars weighed down the bent branches. I talked on, waving my arms. The fingers of the future aeronautical engineer trembled in my grasp. Waking with difficulty from the trance, he promised to come to see me the following Sunday. Fortified by this promise, I went home to Aunt Bobka's by tram.

The whole week after my visit I imagined myself a banker. I carried out transactions in millions with Singapore and Port Said. I acquired a yacht and sailed in it all alone. On Saturday, I had to wake up from the dream. The following day little Borgman was to pay us a visit. Not a single thing I had told him was true. The truth was much more astounding than my inventions, but at the age of twelve I had no idea of how to deal with the truth. My grandfather, Levi Itzkhok, the former rabbi who had been run out of his home town because he had forged Count Branicki's signature on some promissory notes, was a madman in the eyes of the neighbors and the boys on our street. As for Uncle Simon Wolf, I could not bear the loud oddities of that fiery tyrant. Aunt Bobka was the only member of the family one could get along with. Bobka was proud that

I had a banker's son for a friend. She decided that this friendship had laid the foundation for my career, and she baked a jam strudel and a poppy-seed cake for the guest. The heart of our race, the heart that faces struggle with such endurance, was in these pastries. Grandfather, with his broken top hat and rags wrapped round his swollen feet, we bundled off to the neighbors, the Appelkhots, and I made him promise that he would not turn up until the guest was gone. We also managed to dispose of Simon Wolf. He went off to the Bear to drink tea with his disreputable friends, and as they served vodka there too, we could count on not seeing him back soon.

Here I ought to explain that the family from which I come did not resemble other Jewish families. There were drunkards among us and men who seduced generals' daughters and left them before reaching the frontier, and Grandfather forged signatures and composed letters that deserted women used for blackmailing purposes.

I had done my utmost to keep Simon Wolf away the whole day. I gave him three roubles I had saved up. It takes time to spend three roubles, Simon Wolf would come home late and the banker's son would never know that my tales of uncle's strength and kindness were made out of whole cloth. Looked at with the insight of the heart, they were not really lies, but a cursory glance at filthy, loudmouthed Simon Wolf might make it difficult to discover this inscrutable truth about him.

On Sunday morning Aunt Bobka got into a brown woolen dress. Her fat, kindly breasts spread in all directions. Then she put on a print kerchief with flowers, the kerchief worn to synagogue on the Day of Atonement and Rosh Hashana. Aunt Bobka placed the pastries, the jam, the crescents on the table, and waited.

We lived in a basement. Borgman raised his eyebrows as he walked along the humpbacked passage. A barrel of water stood in the entry. No sooner did Borgman come in than I began to entertain him with all sorts of marvels. I showed him an alarm clock which Grandfather had made with his own hands to the last screw. A lamp was attached to the clock; at the half-hour and the hour the lamp lit up. I also showed him a jar of shoe polish, made up according to Levi Itzkhok's formula, the secret of which he had divulged to no one. Then Borgman and I read several pages of Grandfather's manuscript. It was written in Yiddish, on square yellow sheets as big as maps. The manuscript was entitled "The Headless Man." It contained a description of all of the author's neighbors during his entire lifetime, first at Skvira and Belaya Tzerkov, then in Odessa. Undertakers, cantors, Jewish drunkards, female cooks who prepared the feasts at *briths* and the rascals who performed the ritual operation, such were his heroes

— all worthless people, stutterers, with misshapen rumps, knobby noses, pimples on their bald pates.

During the reading, Aunt Bobka, in her brown dress, appeared on the scene. Ensphered in her fat kindly bosom, she floated across the room with a samovar on a tray. I introduced them. Bobka said: "Pleased to meet you," held out her stiff, sweaty fingers and scraped both her feet. Everything was going very well, couldn't have gone better. The Appelkhots kept a tight hold on Grandfather. I dragged out his treasures one after another: grammars of every language in the world and the sixty-six volumes of the Talmud. Mark was dazzled by the jar of shoe polish, the remarkable alarm clock and the mountainous Talmud — all objects that could not be seen in any other house.

We had two glasses of tea apiece with the strudel, and then Bobka, wagging her head and backing out of the room, disappeared. My spirits having risen, I struck a pose and began to recite the lines that I loved above all else in the world. Antony stands over Caesar's corpse and addresses the Roman people:

> Friends, Romans, countrymen, lend me your ears;
> I come to bury Caesar, not to praise him.

Thus does Antony open his speech. I choked and pressed my hands to my breast:

> He was my friend, faithful and just to me:
> But Brutus says he was ambitious;
> And Brutus is an honorable man.
> He hath brought many captives home to Rome,

Whose ransoms did the general coffers fill:
Did this in Caesar seem ambitious?
When that the poor have cried, Caesar has wept:
Ambition should be made of sterner stuff:
Yet Brutus says he was ambitious;
And Brutus is an honorable man.
You all did see that on the Lupercal
I thrice presented him a kingly crown,
Which he did thrice refuse: was this ambition?
Yet Brutus says he was ambitious;
And, sure, he is an honorable man.

Before my eyes, in a hazy universe, was suspended Brutus' face. It grew whiter than chalk. The Roman populace, muttering, surged toward me. I raised my arm — Borgman's eyes obediently followed it. I raised my arm, my clenched fist trembled — and through the window I caught sight of Uncle Simon Wolf crossing the yard in the company of redheaded Leykakh, the old-clothes man. They were carrying a hatrack of reindeer antlers and a red chest with pendant ornaments in the shape of lions' gaping jaws. Bobka, too, saw him through the window. Heedless of the visitor, she flew into the room and, clutching me with her little hands, sobbed out:

"Oh, my darling, he's been buying furniture again!"

Little Borgman in his schoolboy uniform rose and bowed to Bobka, nonplussed. Someone was trying to break into the room. In the passage outside there was the sound of clumping and of a chest being dragged along the floor. The thunderous voices of

Simon Wolf and redheaded Leykakh were deafening. Both were tipsy.

"Bobka," shouted Simon Wolf, "try and guess how much I gave for these antlers. . . ."

He blared like a trumpet, but there was a note of uncertainty in his voice. Though drunk, Simon Wolf knew how we all hated redheaded Leykakh, who prodded him to make all these purchases which filled the house to overflowing with useless, absurd furniture.

Bobka held her peace. Leykakh said something to Simon Wolf in a whisper. To drown out his snake-like hissing, to allay my own anguish, I shouted Antony's words:

> But yesterday the word of Caesar might
> Have stood against the world: now lies he there,
> And none so poor to do him reverence.
> O masters, if I were disposed to stir
> Your minds and hearts to mutiny and rage,
> I should do Brutus wrong and Cassius wrong,
> Who, you all know, are honorable men.

At that moment there was a crash. It was Bobka knocked down by a blow from her husband. She must have made a biting remark about the antlers. The daily scene began. Simon Wolf's coppery voice calked all the chinks and crannies of the universe. He used the same language as always.

"You suck my blood," he thundered accusingly, "you suck my blood to fill your beastly bellies. . . . The work is killing me. I have nothing to work with any more, no hands, no feet . . . you've tied a stone round my neck, there's a stone hanging round my neck. . . ."

Cursing me and Bobka with Jewish curses, he wished it on us that our eyes should melt out of their sockets, that our children should start rotting in their mother's womb, that we should have no time to bury each other and be dragged by the hair to a common grave.

Little Borgman rose from his seat. He was pale and looked about him helplessly. He did not understand the idioms of Jewish profanity, but with Russian obscenities he was familiar, and Simon Wolf wasn't above using these too. The banker's son stood twisting his cap in his hands. I saw two little Borgmans instead of one, and I tried to shout down all the evil of this world. My agony and Caesar's death were one. I was dead and I shouted. The words rose hoarsely from the very bottom of my being.

If you have tears, prepare to shed them now.
You all do know this mantle: I remember
The first time ever Caesar put it on;
'Twas on a summer's evening, in his tent,
That day he overcame the Nervii:
Look, in this place ran Cassius' dagger through:
See what a rent the envious Casca made:
Through this the well-beloved Brutus stabb'd;
And as he pluck'd his cursed steel away,
Mark how the blood of Caesar follow'd it.

Yet nothing could drown out Simon Wolf's voice.

Bobka sat on the floor, sobbing and blowing her nose. The imperturbable Leykakh was moving the chest about behind the partition. At that point my crazy grandfather got it into his head to come to my assistance. He broke away from the Appelkhots, crept up to the window and started sawing away at his fiddle, no doubt in order to keep the neighbors from hearing Simon Wolf's curses. Borgman looked at the window, which was level with the courtyard, and reeled back in horror. My poor grandfather's rigid blue face was contorted in a grimace; he wore a dented high hat, a black quilted robe with bone buttons, and broken shoes on his elephantine feet. His tobacco-stained beard hung in tufts that floated in the wind. Mark fled.

"It's all right," he muttered, rushing out of the room, "it's all right, really. . . ."

His little uniform and his cap with turned-up edges flashed through the courtyard.

With his departure I calmed down. I was all resolution and composure. I was waiting for night. When Grandfather went to bed, having covered his square sheet with Hebrew pothooks – he was describing the Appelkhots with whom he had spent the day, thanks to me — I made my way into the passage. It had an earthen floor. I moved in the dark, barefoot, wearing a long, patched nightshirt. Through the cracks in the boards the cobblestones glimmered with sharp splinters of light. In the corner as usual stood the water barrel. I lowered myself into it. The water cut me in two. I put my head under water, choked, and rose to the surface. From a shelf a cat gazed at me sleepily. The second time I stayed under longer. The water gurgled round me, my groans screwed themselves into it. I opened my eyes and at the bottom of the barrel I saw my shirt like a sail and two small legs pressed close together. Again I weakened, and rose to the surface. Beside the barrel stood my grandfather in his nightshirt. His one tooth rang.

"My grandson," he spoke clearly and contemptuously, "I'm taking a dose of castor oil, so as to have something to place on your grave. . . ."

I cried out, beside myself, and violently plunged into the water. Grandfather's feeble hand pulled me out. Then, for the first time that day, I wept, and the world of tears was so great and beautiful, that those tears blotted everything else from my eyes.

I came to in bed, wrapped in quilts. Grandfather was pacing the room, whistling. Fat Aunt Bobka was warming my hands in her bosom. I surrendered them to her.

"How he shivers, our little fool, our child," she said. "Where does he find the strength to shiver so?"

Grandfather plucked at his beard, whistled and went on pacing the room. Behind the wall Simon Wolf snored, exhaling painfully. Having battled all day, he slept soundly all night.

The Awakening

ALL the people in our circle – brokers, shopkeepers, bank clerks and shipping company employes – had their children taught music. It was simply a mania. Our fathers, aware of being failures, instituted a lottery. They built it on the bones of children. Odessa, to a greater degree than other cities, was possessed by this craze. And indeed, in the course of decades, our town supplied the concert stages of the world with child prodigies. Mischa Elman, Zimbalist, Gabrilowitsch, all came from Odessa, and it was there that Jascha Heifetz made his début.

When a boy reached the age of four or five, his mother would take the puny little creature to Mr. Zagursky. Zagursky ran a child prodigy factory, a factory of Jewish dwarfs in lace collars and patent leather shoes. He ferreted them out of the slums of Moldavanka and the stinking courtyards of the Old Market. Zagursky gave the prodigies the initial training, then they were dispatched to Professor Auer in Petersburg. Mighty harmonies dwelt in the souls of some of these wizened starvelings with blue swollen heads. They became celebrated virtuosos.

And so my father decided to enter me, too, in the race. Although I had already outgrown the age of child prodigies – I was going on fourteen – I was so undersized and delicate that I could easily be passed off as an eight-year-old. In that lay all his hope.

I was taken to see Zagursky. Out of respect for my grandfather, he agreed to charge no more than one rouble a lesson – a modest fee. My grandfather, Levi Itzkhok, was the laughing stock of the town as well as its pride. Wearing a top hat and broken shoes, he strode up and down the streets, settling the knottiest problems. He would be asked what a gobelin was, why the Jacobins betrayed Robespierre, how artificial silk was made, what a Caesarean operation was. My grandfather knew all the answers. So, out of deference to his learning and madness, Zagursky charged us one rouble a lesson. Besides, it was only because he was afraid of Grandfather that he had taken me on at all, for there was nothing in me to warrant it. The notes that came from my violin were like iron filings. These sounds lacerated my own heart, but Father would not give up. At home the talk was always of Mischa Elman, whom the Czar himself had exempted from military service. Zimbalist, according to Father's information, had been presented to the King of England and had played at Buckingham Palace. Gabrilowitsch's parents had purchased two houses in Petersburg. The child prodigies brought fortunes to their parents. My father would have put up with poverty, but he could not do without glory.

"It is impossible," whispered in his ear those who dined at his expense, "it is impossible that the grandchild of such a grandfather shouldn't . . ."

My mind, however, was turned in a different direction. When I was doing my violin exercises, I would place a volume by Turgenev or Dumas on the music stand and while scraping away, God knows how, I devoured page after page. In the daytime I would tell the boys of the quarter fabulous yarns, and during the night I would transfer them to paper. Authorship was a hereditary occupation in our family. All his life Levi Itzkhok worked on a tale entitled "The Headless Man." I took after him.

Weighed down by music and a violin case, three times a week I would trudge to Witte Street, formerly Dvoryanskaya Street, where Zagursky lived. There, along the walls, waiting their turn, sat Jewish women, wrought up to the pitch of hysteria. They pressed against their feeble knees violin cases larger than the artists who were destined to play at Buckingham Palace.

The door of the sanctum would open. Big-headed, freckled children with necks like the stems of flowers and a consumptive flush on their cheeks would stagger out of Zagursky's study. The door would slam to, swallowing another dwarf. Behind the wall the professor, distinguished by a flowing tie and carroty locks, sang, waved his baton and teetered on his thin legs. Manager of the monstrous lottery, in his fits of inspiration he peopled Moldavanka and the black holes of the Old Market with ghosts of pizzicati and cantilenas. The arias were later polished to a diabolical sparkle by old Professor Auer.

I didn't fit into this sect. A dwarf, like the rest of them, I heard another summons in the ancestral voice.

The first step was difficult. One day I left the house carrying the violin, the music and twelve roubles – payment for a month's lessons. I was walking down Nezhin Street and to get to Zagursky's I had to turn into Witte Street. But instead I walked up Tiraspol Street and found myself at the waterfront. My study hours flew by in the Pratique Harbor. Thus began my liberation. Zagursky's studio never saw me again. More important matters occupied my mind. My schoolmate Nemanov and I fell into the habit of going aboard the steamer "Kensington" to visit a sailor by the name of Trotteyburn. Nemanov was a year younger than I, but ever since he had turned eight he had occupied himself with commerce. He had a genius for business and eventually fulfilled the promise he gave as a boy. He is now a New York millionaire, a director of General Motors, a corporation as powerful as Ford. Nemanov took me with him because I silently obeyed his orders. From Mr. Trotteyburn he bought pipes that had been smuggled in as contraband. These pipes were made by the old sailor's brother in Lincoln.

"Gentlemen," Mr. Trotteyburn would say to us, "mark my word, you should use your own hands to shape your darlings. . . . To smoke a factory-made pipe is like putting an enema into your mouth. . . . Have you ever heard of Benvenuto Cellini? He was a master craftsman. My brother who lives in Lincoln could tell you a thing or two about him. My brother doesn't interfere with anybody. His one conviction is that you should shape your darlings with your own hands. . . . We can't help sharing his opinion, gentlemen. . . ."

Nemanov sold the pipes to bankers, foreign consuls, wealthy Greeks. He made one hundred per cent profit on them.

The pipes of the Lincoln master breathed poetry. There was an idea in each one of them, a drop of eternity. A little yellow eye glowed in the mouthpiece, the cases were lined with satin. I tried to imagine how Matthew Trotteyburn lived in old England, the last pipe master, a man who swam against the current.

"We can't help agreeing, gentlemen, that you must shape your darlings with your own hands. . . ."

The ponderous waves beating against the jetty bore me further and further away from our house reeking of onions and the Jewish fate. From the harbor I moved to a point beyond the breakwater. There, on a bit of sandy beach the boys from Primorskaya Street had their hangout. From morning till night they did not put their pants on, but were diving under barges, stealing cocoanuts for their dinner and waiting for the days when freight boats would start coming in from Kherson and Kamenka, laden with watermelons which one could split open against the mooring posts.

Swimming became my dream. I was ashamed to confess to these bronzed urchins that, though born in Odessa, I had not seen the sea until I was ten, and that at fourteen I did not know how to swim.

How late in life I had to learn the essential things! In my childhood, nailed to the Talmud, I led the life of a sage; having grown up, I began to climb trees.

Swimming proved an impossible attainment. The hydrophobia of the Spanish rabbis and Frankfort money-changers who were my ancestors, dragged me to the bottom. The water simply refused to hold me up. Battered and full of sea water, I would return to my violin and music. I was bound to the instruments of my crime and lugged them about with me.

The contest between the rabbis and the sea continued until the moment when the local sea god, Yefim Nikitich Smolich, a proofreader on the *Odessa News,* took pity on me. There was a warm spot for Jewish boys in his athletic breast. He presided over a horde of rachitic starvelings. He collected them in the bug-infested slums of the Moldavanka, took them to the seashore, dug them into the sand, did gymnastic exercises with them, dived with them, taught them songs, and while baking in direct sunlight, he told them stories about fishes and other creatures. To grownups Nikitich would say that he was a naturalist. Listening to his tales, the Jewish children would laugh heartily, and squeal and fawn on him like puppies. The sun sprinkled them with creeping freckles, the color of lizards.

The old man had watched my duel with the waves from the corner of his eyes, without saying a word. When he noticed that I had given up hope and that I wasn't going to learn how to swim unaided, he included me among his heart's tenants. It was wholly ours, his gay heart, free of all ambition, greed and anxiety.

With his copper-colored shoulders, head of an old gladiator, and tanned, slightly bandy legs, this sovereign of waters polluted with kerosene and watermelon rind would lie on the beach beyond the breakwater among us, the offscourings of a race that does not know how to die. I loved this man with a love that only a boy suffering from hysteria and headaches can conceive for an athlete. I always tagged after him and tried to be of service to him.

He would say to me: "Don't get flustered. Strengthen your nerves. Swimming will come of itself. What is this about the water not holding you up? Why shouldn't it hold you up?"

Seeing my earnestness, Nikitich singled me out of his entire following and made an exception in my favor. He invited me to his attic. It was spacious and clean and spread with straw mats. He showed me his dogs, his pigeons, his hedgehog and tortoise. In return for these marvels I brought him a tragedy from my pen.

"I knew you scribbled," said Nikitich. "One can see it by your eyes. . . . Most of the time you don't look at anything. . . ."

He read my writings, shrugged his shoulders, passed his hand over his gray curly hair and paced the attic.

"I believe there is a divine spark in you. . . ." he drawled, pausing after each word.

We went out into the street. The old man halted, brought down his stick on the sidewalk full force and stared at me.

"What is it that you lack? It isn't that you're too young – you'll get over that in time. What you lack is a feeling for nature. He pointed his stick to a tree with a reddish trunk and a low crown:

"What tree is that?"

I did not know.

"What grows on that bush?"

I did not know that either. We were crossing the little park that juts into the Alexandrovsky Prospekt. The old man kept pointing his stick at all the trees, he seized me by the shoulders when a bird flew by and made me listen to its call.

"What bird is that?"

I did not know the answers. The names of trees

and their classification, the names of birds and where they migrated, the points where the sun rose and set, when the dew was heaviest – of all that I knew nothing.

"And you dare write? A man who does not live in contact with nature, as an animal or a rock does, will not write two lines worth a row of pins in his life. Your landscapes are like descriptions of stage sets. What the devil have your parents been thinking of these fourteen years?"

What had they been thinking of? Of notes falling due, of Mischa Elman's mansions. . . . But I didn't tell this to Nikitich, I held my peace.

At home I did not touch my dinner. I couldn't eat.

A feeling for nature, I said to myself. My God, why hadn't I thought of it? Where could I find a person who would tell me about bird calls and the names of trees? What do I know about them? I could recognize lilac, and that only when in blossom. Lilac and acacia. De Ribas and Greek Street were lined with acacias.

At dinner father told a new story about Jascha Heifetz. He had heard it from Mendelsohn, Jascha's uncle, whom he had run into near Robinat's. It appears that the boy gets eight hundred roubles for an appearance. Figure out how much that would make at the rate of fifteen concerts a month.

I figured it out: it came to twelve thousand roubles a month. While I was doing the multiplication and carrying four, I glanced out of the window. Across the small concrete courtyard Mr. Zagursky, my music teacher, was advancing solemnly, leaning on a stick. He wore a cloak which floated gently in the wind and his reddish curls peeped out from under his soft felt hat. It could not be said that he had been too prompt in taking notice of my defection. Over three months had elapsed since my violin came to rest on the sand near the breakwater. . . .

Zagursky was approaching the main entrance. I made a dash for the back door, but this had been nailed up the day before as a precaution against thieves. There was no escape. I locked myself in the toilet. Half an hour later the entire family gathered near the toilet door. The women were weeping. My aunt Bobka rubbed her fat shoulder against the door and sobbed chokingly. My father was silent. When he broke his silence, he spoke in a voice that was extraordinarily low and distinct:

"I am an officer," he said. "I own an estate. I go hunting. The peasants pay me rent. I have placed my son in the Corps of Cadets. I don't have to worry about my son. . . ."

He grew silent. The women were sniffling. Then a terrific blow landed on the toilet door. My father pounded it with his whole body, and then flew at it on the run.

"I am an officer," he yelled, "I go hunting . . . I'll kill him . . . it's the end. . . ."

The hook came off the door, but there was still a bolt which held by a single nail. The women were rolling on the floor, screaming; they clutched at my father's legs; maddened, he tried to shake himself free. Attracted by the noise, his mother, an old woman, reached the scene.

"My child," she said to him in Yiddish, "our sorrow is great. It has no limit. Only bloodshed is lacking in our house. I do not wish to see bloodshed in our house. . . ."

Father groaned. I heard him walk away with a shambling gait. The bolt still hung by a single nail. I stayed in my fortress till late at night. When everybody had gone to bed, my aunt Bobka took me to my grandmother's. It was a long walk. Moonlight lay motionless on unknown bushes, on nameless trees. An invisible bird called, then ceased; perhaps it fell asleep. What bird was it? What was its name? Does the dew fall in the evening? Where is the constellation of the Big Dipper? Where does the sun rise?

We were walking along Pochtovaya Street. Bobka firmly held me by the hand to prevent my running away. She was right. I was thinking of running away.

The Revolution

—

Gedali

On Sabbath eves the thick sadness of memories torments me. On such evenings, long ago, my grandfather used to stroke the volumes of Ibn Ezra with his yellow beard. My grandmother, in a lace kerchief, would make magic over the Sabbath candles with her knotty fingers and sob sweetly. On those evenings my childish heart would rock like a little ship on enchanted waves. Oh, the moldered Talmuds of my childhood! Oh, the thick sadness of memories!

I roam through Zhitomir looking for a shy star. Beside the ancient synagogue, beside its yellow and indifferent walls, old Jews sell chalk, wicks, washing blue – Jews with prophets' beards and passionate rags on their sunken chests.

Here, before me, is the market place and the death of the market place. Killed is the fat soul of abundance. Dumb padlocks hang on the stalls and the granite of the pavement is as clean as the bald spot of a dead man. The shy star twinkles and goes out.

Success came to me later, success came just before

sunset. Gedali's shop was tucked away in a row of closed stores. Dickens, where was your friendly shade that day? You would have seen in this old curiosity shop a pair of gilt slippers and ships' cables, an ancient compass and a stuffed eagle, a Winchester with the date 1810 engraved on it and a battered saucepan.

Old Gedali, the proprietor, walks around his treasures in the pink vacuum of evening, a little man in dark glasses and a green frock coat that reaches to the floor. He rubs his small white hands, plucks at his little gray beard and, cocking his head, listens to invisible voices that float down to him.

This shop resembles the treasure box of a solemn boy with a craving for knowledge who will grow up to be a professor of botany. There are buttons in it and a dead butterfly, and the name of its tiny proprietor is Gedali. Everyone has left the market place, Gedali has stayed on. He slips in and out of a labyrinth of globes, skulls and dead flowers, waving a bright duster of cock's feathers and flicking the dust off flowers that have died.

And now we sit on two empty beer barrels. Gedali twists and untwists his scanty beard. His high hat sways above us like a little black tower. Warm air floats past us. The sky changes color. Up above gentle blood flows from an overturned bottle, and a light odor of decay enfolds me.

"The Revolution — let us say aye to it, but are we to say nay to the Sabbath?" thus Gedali begins, winding about me the silken thongs of his cloudy eyes. "I cry yes to the Revolution; I cry yes to her, but she hides from Gedali and her only messengers are bullets. . . ."

"Sunlight does not enter closed eyes," I answer the old man. "But we will rip open the eyes that are closed."

"The Pole has closed my eyes," the old man says in a barely audible whisper. "The Pole, vicious dog that he is. He takes the Jew and tears out his beard, the cur! And now the vicious dog is getting a beating himself. That's fine, that's – Revolution. And then those who have given the Pole a beating say to me: 'Turn your gramophone over to us, Gedali, we're going to register it.' 'But I love music, madam,' I say to the Revolution. 'You don't know what you love, Gedali; I'm going to shoot you, and then you'll know. And I can't help shooting because I am the Revolution.' "

"She can't help shooting, Gedali," I say to the old man, "because she is the Revolution."

"But the Pole did his shooting, kind sir, because he was the Counterrevolution; you shoot because you are the Revolution. But surely the Revolution is joy. And joy doesn't like orphans in the house. Good deeds are done by good men. Revolution is the good deeds of good men. But good men do not kill. So it is bad men that are making the Revolution. But Poles, too, are bad men. Who, then, will tell Gedali which is Revolution and which is Counterrevolution.

I used to study the Talmud, I love Rashi's commentaries and the books of Maimonides. And there are yet other men of understanding in Zhitomir. And here all of us, learned men, fall upon our faces and cry out at the top of our voices: 'Woe unto us, where is our sweet Revolution?' "

The old man fell silent. And we beheld the first star peeping along the Milky Way.

"The Sabbath has begun," Gedali brought out solemnly; "time for Jews to go to synagogue. . . . Mr. Comrade," he said, rising, and his high hat, like a black tower, swayed on his head, "bring a few good men to Zhitomir. Oh, they are scarce in our town, oh, how scarce! Bring good men and we'll turn all our gramophones over to them. We are no dunces. The International – we know what the International is. I want an International of good men, I want to have every soul registered and given the biggest ration. There, soul, take your fill, please, and enjoy life. The International, Mr. Comrade, you're the one who doesn't know what sauce goes with it."

"Gunpowder's the sauce that goes with it and it's spiced with the best blood. . . ."

And lo! the young Sabbath ascended its throne, coming out of the blue darkness.

"Gedali," I said, "today is Friday and it's already evening. Where can you get a Jewish cookie, a Jewish glass of tea and in the glass of tea a little taste of that God who has been pensioned off?"

"Nowhere," Gedali answered me, hanging the padlock on his little treasure box, "nowhere. There is a tavern next door, and good people used to run it, but nobody eats there nowadays, they just weep."

He buttoned three bone buttons of his green frock coat, flicked himself with the cock's feathers, sprinkled a little water on his soft palms, and was gone – a tiny, lonely dreamer in a black top hat and with a large prayer book under his arm.

The Sabbath has begun. Gedali, founder of a Utopian International, has gone to synagogue to pray.

The Rabbi

". . . All are mortal. The mother alone is destined to eternal life. And when she passes on, she leaves a memory behind which no one as yet has dared to sully. The memory of the mother feeds our compassion even as the ocean, the boundless ocean feeds the rivers that carve the world. . . ."

Those were Gedali's words. He uttered them solemnly. The evening that was being snuffed out ensphered him in the pink haze of its sadness. The old man went on:

"The doors and windows of Hasidism, that passionate edifice, are smashed, but it is as deathless as the mother's soul. With empty eye sockets Hasidism still stands firmly at the crossroads swept by history's fierce winds."

Thus spoke Gedali and, having said his prayers in the synagogue, took me to see Rabbi Motele, the last of the Chernobyl dynasty.

Gedali and I walked up the main street. White churches gleamed in the distance like buckwheat fields. The wheel of a gun carriage groaned round the corner. Two pregnant Ukrainian women came out of a gateway, their coin necklaces jingling, and sat down on a bench. A shy star began to gleam on the sunset's orange battlefield, and peace, Sabbath peace, rested upon the crooked roofs of the Zhitomir ghetto.

"Here," whispered Gedali, pointing to a sprawling house with a shattered façade.

We entered a room, as stony and naked as a morgue. Rabbi Motele sat at a table, surrounded by liars and madmen. He wore a sable *strammel* and a white robe belted with rope. He sat with closed eyes, digging his thin fingers into the yellow down of his beard.

"Where does the Jew come from?" he asked, and raised his eyelids.

"From Odessa," I answered.

"A pious city," said the Rabbi with unusual vehemence, "the star of our exile and, against its will, the well of our misfortunes. What is the Jew's occupation?"

"I put the adventures of Hersh of Ostropol into verse."

"A mighty and worthy task," murmured the Rabbi and dropped his eyelids. "The jackal howls when he is hungry, every fool has folly enough to be despondent, and alone the wise man rends the veil of being with laughter. . . . What did the Jew study?"

"The Torah."

"What is the Jew seeking?"

"Joy."

"Reb Mordkhe," said the zaddik, and shook his beard, "let the young man be seated at the table, let him eat with other Jews, this Sabbath eve, let him rejoice that he is alive and not dead, let him clap his hands when his neighbors dance, let him drink wine if he is given wine."

And Reb Mordkhe, an old buffoon, a hunchbacked old man, no taller than a boy of ten, with everted eyelids, darted up to me.

"Oh, my dear and so very young man," said the ragged Reb Mordkhe and winked at me, "how many rich fools have I known in Odessa, and how many penniless sages have I known in Odessa! Sit down at the table, young man, and drink the wine that won't be offered you. . . ."

We all seated ourselves side by side, the liars, the madmen and the loafers. In the corner brawny Jews who looked like fishermen and apostles moaned over their prayer books. Gedali in his green frock coat was dozing against the wall like a bright-feathered bird. And suddenly behind his back I caught sight of a youth, a youth with the look of Spinoza, with Spinoza's powerful brow and with the sickly face of a nun. He was smoking and shivering, like an escaped prisoner whom his captors had brought back to his cell. Ragged Mordkhe stole up to him from behind, snatched the cigarette from his mouth and ran to my side.

"That's Ilya, the rabbi's son," Mordkhe muttered hoarsely, and brought closer to me the bleeding flesh of his everted eyelids. "The accursed son, the last son, the disobedient son."

And Mordkhe shook his little fist threateningly at the youth and spat in his face.

"Blessed be the Lord," rang out the voice of Rabbi Motele Bratzlavsky, and he broke the bread with his monkish fingers. "Blessed be the God of Israel who has chosen us from among all the nations of the earth. . . ."

The Rabbi blessed the food, and we sat down to eat. Beyond the window horses were neighing and Cossacks were shouting. The wilderness of war yawned beyond the window. The rabbi's son smoked one cigarette after another, through prayers and silence. When supper was over, I was the first to get up.

"My dear and so very young man," mumbled Mordkhe behind my back and tugged my belt, "if there were nobody in the world except the wicked rich and the penniless tramps, how would the saintly live?"

I gave the old man some money and went out into the street. I parted from Gedali and made my way back to the depot. In the propaganda train of the First Cavalry Corps there awaited me the glare of hundreds of lights, the magical brilliance of the radio station, the persistent pounding of printing presses, and my unfinished story for the paper, "The Red Cavalry Man."

The Rabbi's Son

. . . Do you remember Zhitomir, Vasily? Do you remember the Teterev, Vasily, and that evening when the Sabbath, the young Sabbath tripped stealthily along the sunset, her little red heel treading on the stars?

The slender horn of the moon bathed its arrows in the black waters of the Teterev. Funny little Gedali, founder of the Fourth International, was taking us to Rabbi Motele Bratzlavsky's for evening service. Funny little Gedali swayed the cock's feathers of his high hat in the red haze of the evening. The candles in the Rabbi's room blinked their predatory eyes. Bent over prayer books, brawny Jews were moaning in muffled voices, and the old buffoon of the zaddiks of Chernobyl jingled coppers in his torn pocket. . . .

. . . Do you remember that night, Vasily? Beyond the windows horses were neighing and Cossacks were shouting. The wilderness of war was yawning beyond the windows, and Rabbi Motele Bratzlavsky was praying at the eastern wall, his decayed fingers clinging to his *tales*. Then the curtain of the ark was drawn aside, and in the funereal light of the candles we saw the scrolls of the Torah gowned in purple velvet and light blue silk, and suspended above the Torahs the lifeless face, meek and beautiful, of Ilya, the Rabbi's son, the last prince of the dynasty. . . .

Well, the day before yesterday, Vasily, the regiments of the Twelfth Army left the front at Kovel exposed. The victors' scornful cannonade thunderously broke out in the city. Our troops faltered and were thrown into confusion. The propaganda train started crawling away across the field's dead back. And a monstrous Russia in bast shoes shuffled past on either side of the cars, as incredible as a herd of lice. A typhus-ridden peasant mob trudged along, carrying on its shoulders the usual hump of soldiers' death. They jumped on the steps of our train and dropped off, knocked down by butt ends of rifles. They grunted, scratched themselves and moved on in silence.

At the twelfth verst, having run out of potatoes, I tossed a batch of Trotsky's leaflets down to them. But only one of them stretched out a dirty, dead hand for a leaflet. And I recognized Ilya, the son of the rabbi of Zhitomir. I recognized him at once, Vasily. And it was so painful to see the prince, trouserless and doubled up under his soldier's pack, that, in defiance of the rules, we pulled him into our car. His bare knees, as helpless as a woman's, knocked against the rusty iron of the steps; two full-breasted typists in sailor suits dragged the long, bashful body of the dying man along the floor. We laid him on the floor of the editorial office. Cossacks, in red loose trousers, straightened what was left of his clothes. The girls, bearing down on their bandy legs, the legs of simple-minded females, stared drily at his private parts, the tender curly maleness of a spent Semite. And I who had seen him one night during my wanderings began to collect in a little box the scattered belongings of Bratzlavsky, Red Army man. There were all sorts of things here, helter-skelter – the instructions of a propagandist and the notebooks of a Jewish poet. Portraits of Lenin and Maimonides lay side by side: the gnarled iron of Lenin's skull and the dull silk of Maimonides' likeness. A lock of woman's hair lay in a volume of the resolutions of the Sixth Congress of the Party, and crooked lines of Hebrew verse crowded the margins of Communist leaflets. Like a sad and niggardly rain they fell upon me – pages from the Song of Songs and revolver cartridges. The sad rain of sunset washed my dusty hair, and I said to the youth who lay there dying on a torn mattress:

"One Friday evening four months ago, Gedali who owns the curiosity shop took me to your father, Rabbi Motele, but you were not a member of the Party then, Bratzlavsky. . . ."

"I was in the Party," the boy answered, scratching his chest and writhing with fever, "but I couldn't leave my mother."

"And now, Ilya?"

"In a revolution a mother is a mere episode," he whispered, growing quieter. "My turn came, and the organization sent me to the front."

"And you found yourself in Kovel, Ilya?"

"I found myself in Kovel," he cried out in despair. "The rats exposed the front. I took command of a scratch regiment, but it was too late. I didn't have enough artillery."

He died before we reached Rovno. He died, the last prince, in the midst of verses, phylacteries and foot-clouts. We buried him near a forgotten railway station. And I, who am hardly able to hold the tempests of my imagination within this immemorial body, I was with my brother as he breathed his last.

Karl Yankel

When I was a boy there was a smithy in the Peresyp section of Odessa owned by Yoyna Brutman. It was the haunt of horse dealers, carters, and butchers from the municipal slaughterhouses. The smithy stood on the Balta Road. By making it your observation post you could intercept the peasants bringing oats and Bessarabian wine to the city markets. Yoyna was a timorous little man, but given to drinking, and the soul of the Odessa Jew lived in him.

In my day he had three growing sons. They had the best dovecot in town. The father came up to the waist of the shortest. It was on the Peresyp beach that I first came to ponder the might of the forces that work mysteriously within Nature. Three beefy huskies with purple shoulders and feet the size of shovels would carry wizened old Yoyna down to the water as if he were an infant. Nevertheless it was he and none other who had begotten them. There was no doubt about it. The blacksmith's wife went to synagogue twice a week – Friday evening and Saturday morning; it was a Hasidic one, where they danced on Passover until they were as frenzied as dervishes. Yoyna's wife paid tribute to the emissaries that the Galician zaddiks dispatched to the southern provinces. The blacksmith never interfered where his wife's relations with God were concerned. After work he would go off to a little cellar near the slaughterhouse and there, sipping cheap rosy wine, would listen meekly to the talk of cattle prices and politics.

In size and strength the sons took after the mother. When they grew up, two of them joined the partisans. The elder was killed at Voznesensk; the other Brutman, Semyon, went over to Primakov, attaching himself to the Red Cossack Division. He was elected commander of a regiment, and later, when the division was transformed into an army corps, became a divisional commander. He and a few youths from small towns were the first of the company of Jewish fighters, cavalrymen and partisans, an eminently picturesque and astonishing breed.

The third son followed in his father's footsteps and became a blacksmith. He worked in a plant manufacturing plows. Unlike Semyon, he was not married and begot no children.

Semyon's sons led a nomadic existence, traveling with his division. The old woman, his mother, needed a grandson, to whom she could tell stories about the Baal Shem. She finally achieved a grandson through her younger daughter, Polya. Alone of all the family the girl had taken after her father. She was timid, nearsighted, and had a delicate skin.

Her suitors were many. Polya chose Ovsey Belotzerkovsky. We could not understand her choice. Word that the couple were living happily was even more astonishing. When pots get broken, women have a way of hiding from the world how it happened. In this case it was Ovsey who broke the pots. One year after the marriage he brought suit against his mother-in-law, Brana Brutman. Taking advantage of the fact that Ovsey was out of town and that Polya had gone to the hospital to be treated for an inflammation of the breast, the old woman kidnapped her newborn grandson and bore him off to the flat of Naftula Gerchik, a surgeon of sorts, and there in the presence of ten ruins, ten ancients, habitués of the Hasidic synagogue, the infant was duly circumcised.

The news did not reach Ovsey Belotzerkovsky until he was back in town. His name was down as a candidate for membership in the Party. He decided to seek the advice of Bychach, secretary of the Communist cell of the office of State Trade.

"You've been morally besmirched," Bychach said to him, "you can't let them get away with it."

The office of the Odessa prosecuting attorney decided to turn this trial into a public event and hold it in the Petrovsky Factory. Naftula Gerchik, the *mohel,* and Brana Brutman, age sixty-two, found themselves in the dock.

In Odessa, Naftula was as much of a municipal landmark as the Duc de Richelieu's statue. I remember him passing our windows on Dalnitzky Street carrying a frayed, greasy midwife's bag. The bag contained his simple instruments. He would pull the knife out of it or else a bottle of vodka with a piece of honey cake. He would sniff the cake, down the drink, and then chant the prayers. Naftula was as redheaded as the first redhead on earth. When he had cut off what he should, he did not drain off the blood through a glass tube, but sucked it out with his everted lips. The blood would be smeared all over his unkempt beard. When he came out to the company, he was tipsy. His little bearish eyes shone with mad glee. Redheaded as the first redhead on earth, he would pronounce a nasal blessing over the liquor. With one hand Naftula would tip the vodka into his crooked, fire-breathing hole of a mouth, surrounded by hair, while in the other he would hold out a plate. On it lay the little knife stained with infant blood, and a piece of gauze. Naftula made the round of the company with his plate, collecting money; he pushed his way among the women, fell over them, clutched their breasts and shouted so that the whole street could hear him.

"Mammas, fatties!" the old man shouted, flashing his coral eyes, "turn out boys for Naftula, thresh wheat on your bellies, do your best for redheaded Naftula . . . turn out boys, mammas, you fatties, you!"

The husbands threw money into the plate. The wives wiped the blood off his beard with napkins.

The courtyards of Gluhaya and Gospitalnaya Streets knew no dearth. They were swarming with children, as river mouths with roe. Naftula trudged along with his bag like a tax collector. The prosecuting attorney, Orlov, put a stop to his rounds.

The prosecuting attorney thundered from his rostrum, trying to prove that the surgeon was a cleric. Naftula's tousled head, looking like a chestnut burr, was waggling way below, at the feet of the guards. The old man was eloquent of the genius of the race: in court he dried up, shrank together, diminished incredibly.

"Do you believe in God?" the prosecuting attorney asked him.

"Let him believe in God who won two hundred thousand in the sweepstakes," answered Naftula.

"Weren't you surprised when Citizeness Brutman came to you at such a late hour of the night, in the rain, with a newborn infant in her arms?"

"I am surprised," said Naftula, "when a human being behaves like a human being, but when he acts crazy, I'm not surprised."

These answers failed to satisfy the prosecuting attorney. There was the matter of the glass tube. The prosecuting attorney argued that by sucking out the blood with his lips the defendant exposed tens of thousands of children to the danger of infection. Naftula's head was swaying somewhere in the vicinity of the floor. He sighed, closed his eyes, and wiped his sunken mouth with his fist.

"What are you mumbling there, Citizen Gerchik?" the presiding judge asked him.

Naftula fixed his dull stare on Orlov.

"The late Mosoo Sussman," he said with a sigh, "your late papa, had a head such as you won't find in the whole world. And praise God he didn't get a stroke thirty years ago when he called me for your *briss.* And now we see that you've grown up to be somebody in the Soviet Government and that Naftula didn't clip off a scrap of anything that could possibly be of use to you later. . . ."

He blinked his bearish eyes, shook his red burr of a head, and fell silent. He was answered by salvoes of laughter, thunderous volleys of guffaws. Orlov, né Sussman, waved his arms and shouted something that could not be heard in the cannonade. He demanded that something or other should be put on record. . . . Sasha Svetlov, on the staff of the *Odessa News,* sent him a note from the press section. "Syoma, you're an ass," the note read, "slay him with irony: only laughter kills. Yours, Sasha."

The courtroom quieted down when Belotzerkovsky, the plaintiff, was brought in.

He repeated the charge he had made in writing. A lanky fellow, he wore riding breeches and cavalry boots. The Tiraspol and Balta district committees of the Party had co-operated with him fully in his work of stock-piling cotton seeds. At the height of the campaign he had received a telegram about the birth of his son. After consultation with the chairman of the Balta district committee of the Party, he decided to do no more than send a telegram of congratulation, so as not to interrupt the work. Only two weeks later did he return home. In all, 64,000 poods of cotton seed had been collected in the district. In his flat he found nobody besides the baby and a neighbor, Citizeness Harchenko, a washerwoman by trade, who was present as one of the witnesses. His wife had gone to the hospital, and Citizeness Harchenko was singing a song to the baby and rocking the cradle, which is cultural backwardness. Knowing witness Harchenko to be an alcoholic, he had not considered it necessary to take notice of what she was singing, but he was surprised to hear that she called the boy Yasha, whereas he had directed that his son be called Karl, in honor of our teacher, Karl Marx. On unpinning the baby's diaper, the plaintiff discovered his misfortune.

The prosecuting attorney asked the plaintiff a number of questions. The defense had no questions to ask. The court attendant brought in Polina Belotzerkovskaya, witness. Moving on unsteady feet, she approached the railing. Her face still bore traces of the strain of her recent confinement, and the tender skin of her forehead was beaded with sweat. She looked round at the diminutive smith who had spruced himself up as if for a holiday, wearing a tie and new boots, and at her mother's coppery face with its gray moustache. On being asked what she knew about the case, she made no direct answer.

Instead, she said that her father was a poor man and for forty years had been working in a smithy on the Balta Road. Her mother, she went on, had borne six children, of whom three had died, one son was a Red Commander, the other worked in a factory.

"Mother is very religious," she said, "anybody can see that; she has always been unhappy because her children were unbelievers and she couldn't bear the thought that her grandsons would not be Jews. You must remember the kind of family mother grew up in. . . . Everybody knows what the town of Miedzyboz is like – why, the women there wear wigs to this day. . . ."

"Tell us, Citizeness," a shrill voice interrupted her. Polina broke off, the beads of sweat on her forehead were tinted as though blood had begun to ooze through her delicate skin.

"Citizeness," repeated the voice, which belonged to former Attorney-at-law Samuel Lining.

If the Sanhedrin existed in our day, Lining would be its head. But there is no Sanhedrin, and Lining, who only at the age of twenty-five learned Russian, at the age of forty began writing appeals to the Senate that were no different from talmudic treatises. He had slept through the trial, his jacket covered with ashes. Polya woke him up.

"Will you tell the court," his fishy row of bluish ill-fitting teeth clacked, "if you knew of your husband's decision to name your son Karl?"

"I did."

"What did your mother name him?"

"Yankel."

"And you, what did you call your son?"

"I called him ducky."

"Why ducky?"

"I call all children ducky."

"Let us proceed," said Lining. His teeth fell out, he caught them with his lower lip and put them in place again. "Let us proceed. In the evening when the baby was taken to the defendant, Gerchik, you were away from home, in the hospital. Is that correct?"

"I was in the hospital."

"What hospital were you in?"

"On Nezhin Street, under Dr. Drizo's care."

"Dr. Drizo was treating you?"

"Yes."

"You are quite sure?"

"How could I make a mistake?"

"I wish to submit an affidavit," Lining's lifeless face rose above the table, "which will make it clear to the court that during the period in question Dr. Drizo was away, attending a congress of pediatricians in Kharkov."

The prosecuting attorney had no objection to the admission of this document.

"Let us proceed further," said Lining, his teeth clacking.

Polya leaned her whole weight on the railing of the dock. Her whisper was hardly audible.

"Maybe it wasn't Dr. Drizo," she said, resting against the railing, "I can't remember everything, I'm worn out. . . ."

Lining scratched his yellow beard with a pencil, rubbed his round back against the bench, and shifted his false teeth about.

Asked to produce the health insurance certificate, Polya said that she had lost it.

"Let's proceed further," said the old man.

Polina wiped her forehead with the palm of her hand. Her husband sat on the edge of a bench, apart from the witnesses. He sat up straight, his long legs in cavalry boots tucked under him. The sunlight fell on his face latticed with small and vicious bones.

"I'll find the paper," Polina whispered, and her arms slid off the railing.

At this moment a baby's wail was heard. Behind the door an infant was bawling lustily.

"What are you thinking of, Polya?" old Brana shouted in a thick voice. "The child hasn't been fed since morning, the child is crying itself sick. . . ."

The Red Army soldiers started, and shifted their rifles. Polina was sliding lower and lower, her head fell back and she dropped to the floor. Her arms flew up, waved in the air, and sank.

"Court is adjourned!" announced the presiding judge.

A thunderous din arose in the hall. Ovsey approached his wife on his storklike legs.

"Eh, feed that baby!" someone shouted from the back benches, making a megaphone of his hands.

"It'll be fed," a woman's voice sang out in the distance, "without your help."

"The daughter's in it, and no mistake," said a workman with high cheekbones who sat next to me, "the daughter will get her cut."

"It's a family affair, pal," his neighbor put in. "A dark business. . . . What's done at night can't be undone by daylight."

The sun's oblique rays sliced the hall. The crowd was milling about, breathing fire and sweat. I elbowed my way into the corridor. The door of the Red Little Corner* was ajar. Karl Yankel's grunting and smacking issued thence. In the Corner hung a portrait of Lenin, the one in which he is speaking from an armored car on the square near the Finland Station in Petrograd. The portrait was surrounded by colored diagrams showing the output of the Petrovsky Factory. Along the walls were banners and guns in wooden stands. A workingwoman with Kirghiz features, her head bent, was nursing Karl Yankel. He himself was a chubby individual, five months old, in knitted socks and with a tuft of white hair on his head. Clinging to the Kirghiz woman with his lips, he was purring and thumping his nurse's breast with his clenched fists.

"What a rumpus they raised," said the Kirghiz woman, "there's someone to feed him."

In the room there was also a girl of seventeen with

* A political clubroom and reading room maintained in factories, etc.

a red kerchief and cheeks bulbous as fir cones. She was busy rubbing Karl Yankel's oilcloth diapers dry.

"He'll be a soldier," said the girl, "see how he fights."

The Kirghiz woman, pulling gently at her nipple, withdrew it from Karl Yankel's mouth. He began to growl and in despair threw back his white-tufted head. The woman freed her other breast and offered it to the boy. He glanced at the nipple with his lackluster little eyes, and then they flashed. The Kirghiz woman looked down at Karl Yankel, cocking her black eyes.

"Why a soldier?" she asked, setting the baby's cap straight, "he'll be a flier, he'll take to the clouds. . . ."

The court was again in session.

A duel was now fought between the prosecuting attorney and the experts, whose statements were rather evasive. The public prosecutor, half rising, banged his desk with his fist. Among the spectators in the front rows I could see Galician zaddiks with their sable caps on their knees. They had come to the court because they had read in the Warsaw papers that the Jewish religion was on trial there. Their faces hung in the stormy, dusty sunlight.

"Down with them!" shouted a member of the League of Communist Youth who had made his way to the very rostrum.

The battle was growing fiercer and fiercer.

Karl Yankel, staring at me dully, was sucking the

Kirghiz woman's breast. The woman was slightly pockmarked.

Beyond the window darted the straight streets trod by my childhood and youth: Pushkinskaya Street sped toward the railway station, Malo-Arnautzkaya ran into the park by the seaside.

I had grown up on those streets, and now it was Karl Yankel's turn, but no one had fought over me as they were fighting over him. Hardly anybody had bothered much about me.

"It's impossible," I whispered to myself, "that you should fail to be happy, Karl Yankel. It's impossible for you not to be happier than I. . . ."

About the Author

The only son of a middle-class Jewish family, Isaac Babel was born on July 13, 1894 (New Style), in Moldavanka, an outlying section of Odessa, the great port city on the Black Sea. All his life his birthplace, with its sun and sea, the large Jewish contingent in its heterogeneous population, had a special place in his affections. The city was good for both his spirit and his body, he wrote. Odessa, not Moscow, where he lived as a grown man, was his home. At the very start of his career he declared that it was the only Russian city where "our own Maupassant" could be born.

The boy was taught at home until he was eleven years old, when he was sent to the Nicholas I Commercial School, which offered secondary education. A Jewish boy was more likely to be admitted there than to a *gymnasia*. This was the stormy year of 1905, when the last Romanov granted his subjects a constitution "wrapped in pogroms." The Babels witnessed such a riot, but were spared physical injury, nor were their possessions plundered.

Young Isaac was given traditional instruction in Hebrew by a private tutor and for a while he took music lessons, which proved a total loss. His familiarity with Yiddish and with elements of Jewish folklore he may have owed to his paternal grandmother, who at one time lived with the family. Some of the holy days were observed, certainly the two-day New Year, the Day of Atonement, and Passover, on which occasions the family attended synagogue services. In later years at Passover, a particularly memorable festival, Babel went out of his way to secure *matza* for himself and was glad to accept an invitation to a Seder. On the Day of Atonement he would sometimes go to a synagogue and say a memorial prayer addressed to what had long since become for him ex-God.

At school Isaac conceived a passion for the language and literature of France. We have his word for it that at fifteen he began writing stories—in French. Avid reading and idle hours at the harbor, with its turbulent, exciting life, offered relief from studies. The city boasted a university, but the youth's chances of being admitted to it were less than slim, since the number of Jewish students in the institutions of higher learning was strictly limited. As a result, he entered the less exclusive Business Institute in Kiev. There he became close to the family of a cultivated, well-to-do Jewish manufacturer of agricultural machinery (Babel's father had an agency for these products), and eventually married one of the man's daughters.

Having been exempted from military service as an only son, the youth graduated from the Institute in

1915 and made his way to Leningrad (then Petrograd). The capital was barred to Jews, except for certain privileged groups. Babel had a spurious residence permit and managed to attend some lecture courses, though not at the university. The one fact that is clear about this period in Petrograd is that he did some writing. He peddled several short stories without success. After much hesitation he steeled his heart and in 1916 took two manuscripts to the office of a monthly that Maxim Gorky had launched. In accepting them, the editor held forth on the cruel hardships and the glory of the literary calling, and forthwith consecrated him to it. This talk was the beginning of a life-long friendship, in which the older man played the part less of the mentor than of the protector.

The two stories, Babel's first efforts, appeared in the November issue of the periodical. He never reprinted them, but they are not without interest. One of them is about a Jewish drummer from Odessa who finds himself in a town barred to Jews without a residence permit. The police tell him to leave on the next train. But this would mean the loss of an order he badly needs. He gets out of his predicament by spending the night with a prostitute, the sordid strategem turning out to be a genuine human contact. The piece has characteristics foreshadowing Babel's mature work: extreme concision, telling details, matter-of-fact treatment of venal love, unexpected situations credibly realized. The other narrative (a less successful performance) also deals with sex almost as though it had been written fifty years later in another country. In fact, the author was brought to book for pornography. "The trial was set for March, 1917," he reminisced long afterwards, "but late in February the people, coming to my defense, burned the documents in the case and while they were at it also committed the Circuit Court to the flames."

Babel could not but welcome the liberal regime inaugurated by the Provisional Government—one of its first measures was the abolition of Jewish legal disabilities. He volunteered for the army and saw action on the Rumanian front. By the time the Bolsheviks took power he was out of uniform and back in the old capital. Like many Russian soldiers, he seems to have voted against the continuation of the war with his feet. He now regarded the international hostilities as an unmitigated disaster. "On the Field of Honor" is the wry title of a contribution of his to an Odessa periodical. It consists of a translation of several excerpts from accounts of war experiences written by French privates and officers. The episodes are examples of shocking brutality set down with unflinching realism.

His few journalistic ventures during the months that shook the world indicate that he took a dim view of some aspects of the October Revolution. Thus, in commenting approvingly on the transformation of an Institute for Well-Born Maidens into a Maternity Palace, he rejoices over the fact that the building will not house confiscation and requisition agencies and that the constant talk of arrests will not be heard within those walls. He adds: "To shoulder a rifle and shoot at each other may sometimes be sensible, but this is not all that revolution comes to. Who knows? Maybe it is not revolution at all. To make it possible for children to be born in decent surroundings—that, I know, is real revolution." Again, a 1918 issue of a Petrograd Menshevik newspaper (they were still tolerated) carried a contribution by Babel: an adaptation of one of the facetious tales attributed to Hershele Ostropoler, the semi-legendary jester at a hasidic "court." There was nothing political about the piece, but its appearance in an organ of the opposition to the dictatorship suggests that the author's sympathies were not wholly with the new order. Although he was to work under its aegis, he did not join the Communist Party.

For Babel as a writer of fiction the first two or three years of the Soviet era were a fallow period. Gorky had advised him before resuming work on short stories "to go among people," to participate in the life around him, to lay in a stock of observations and impressions. For a while he was employed in the Commissariat of Education, took part in food requisitioning expeditions and in defending the capital against the forces of General Yudenich. Such activities afforded material for reportage. He became more actively engaged in journalism when, in 1920, a recently married man, he joined the Cavalry Corps of the

Red Army in the capacity of a correspondent of the Southern Branch of the Russian Telegraphic Agency, and a member of the staff of the propaganda sheet printed for the Corps. This Cossack unit was to win renown because of the part it played in the Soviet-Polish war that raged that summer. Babel observed the savage fighting at close range and gained intimate knowledge of the horrors of the Civil War, the fires of which were still smoldering. He came to know men who were poles removed from the people among whom he had spent his childhood and youth. Taking time off from his official duties, he roughly and briefly jotted down his impressions in a diary. Unfortunately, only part of it has been preserved.

Soviet-Polish peace late that year found him in a lamentable state, due to acute asthma. His parents and his wife's family arranged for the couple to live in the Caucasus for the sake of his health. During this interlude, which lasted two or three years, he did some reporting and wrote several tall tales, a kind of epic of the Odessa Jewish underworld that had thrived before the advent of the Soviet regime. They were published in newspapers and magazines between 1921 and 1924 and became immensely popular. Almost simultaneously he was painstakingly at work on stories embodying his experiences in the Cossack Corps. Printed in periodicals in 1923–25, they won an enthusiastic public. With the appearance of a small selection of these pieces in 1925 and, the following year, of a larger volume of war stories under a title

Englished as *Red Cavalry*, Babel became the rage of Moscow, where he had been settled since 1924.

Here was a new and compelling voice, a writer with an intensely personal, idiosyncratic way of perceiving the world and an unfailing ear for living speech. The carefully wrought vignettes, sketches, and miniature stories that make up the book are models of tense, highly charged, dynamic prose, mercilessly and unwontedly frank. The style is explosive and hyperbolic, elliptical and extremely concise, riotous with color, crammed with startling metaphors and similes. Paradoxical enough to border on surrealist imagery, they disrupt habitual associations, suggest connections between utterly diverse things, mate objects and concepts.

It is clear from the first three selections in the part of the present volume entitled "The Revolution," which are taken from *Red Cavalry*, that the stories are concerned not only with the combatant but also, to a lesser extent, with the inhabitants of the ghettos in the Ukrainian and Polish towns that he halts in or passes through. He is no more at home in their moribund world than in the Cossacks' world of exuberance and violence. And yet a special emotional quality attaches to the glimpses of Jewish scenes and figures. Memories of the traditional way of life of which he had known something at home have a firm hold on him. One of his most moving miniatures is lyrical with nostalgia for that past with its God, now "pensioned off." He often focuses on a decrepit synagogue squatting behind scattered hovels, and he devotes a vignette to a burial crypt holding the remains of Rabbi Azrail, "the mouth of God," slain by Cossacks in the seventeenth century. For all his skepticism, Babel is drawn to the realm of the spiritual, so significant for the Jewish ethos. Hence his interest in Hasidism. Not that he idealizes this mystical branch of Judaism, which was not immune from corruption. In one story it is charged with holding in "stifling captivity" a town's population of tavernkeepers, peddlers, and middlemen. But his most lovable character is the dedicated Hasid Gedali, in the story of that name. The author declares that the successful merchant or manufacturer, "jovial, pot-bellied, bubbling like cheap wine," is no longer for him the image of the Jew: he has been replaced by a surviving member of a small-town congregation which, situated in the path of war, has been decimated by the contending armies. He writes of the "bitter pride" he discerns in the bony backs and tragic beards of Galician Jews, of their features chiseled by torment, the "somber grandeur" of their grief. Pity for innocent victims? Yes, and also perhaps consciousness of Jewish history and a kinder view of Jewish identity than emerges from the collection as a whole.

In fine, *Red Cavalry* is a book of great imaginative power, of striking originality throughout, sternly devoted to what is true about human beings. It belongs to the limited number of enduring works of genuine literary quality produced since the Revolution.

Red Cavalry met with no little hostile criticism in the press. The author was taken to task for excessive naturalism, that is, his way of calling a spade a bloody shovel, and for his eccentric style. He was also charged with misinterpreting the Revolution as an elemental force of which he seemed afraid, rather than as a rationally planned program of action, and with failing to do justice to the monolithic heroism of the revolutionary cohorts. Above all, he was accused of having sinned in not stressing "the organizing and educational role played by the Communist Party in the Civil War." In a public statement the general who commanded the Cossack Corps described the book as a "crude, deliberate, and arrogant defamation of the Cossack Cavalry Corps."

Babel was not disturbed by the attacks. In the 1920's the writer's freedom was still tolerated. His standing with the authorities was good enough to allow him to cross the border several times. In fact, in 1927–28, and again in 1932–33, he was granted the privilege of a long sojourn abroad. He stayed with his wife, who in 1925 had settled in France. In 1929 she bore him a daughter, but the previous year, when he returned to Moscow, she had refused to follow him. The baby was called Natasha (Nathalie), though he would have preferred a biblical name. He doted on her and missed her badly. It happened that just when his wife emigrated, his mother and sister also expatriated themselves. Genuinely devoted to both, he maintained contact with them by correspondence.

For a long time he clung to the dream of seeing the family reunited.

Half a dozen years passed before a successor to *Red Cavalry,* entitled *Stories,* came off a Moscow press. This was a miscellany consisting for the most part of material printed, like his earlier work, in periodicals. It contains the pieces dealing with the experiences of a Jewish boy in Odessa before the Revolution. Here, according to Babel, autobiography is modified by a large measure of fiction. The writing is less idiosyncratic and more leisurely, allowing for plot development and some psychologizing. Babel complained that the text of a story called "Karl Yankel" had been "horribly distorted," presumably by censorship. The end, which seems somewhat of a *non sequitur,* may have been tacked on. By this time, it should be noted, the government control of cultural activities was growing increasingly oppressive. The artist was required to use his special skill to promote the policies of the Party and do so in accordance with an officially approved canon. Nothing could be more disheartening to a writer of Babel's gifts and temperament. Furthermore, the political regime had degenerated, he decided, in other ways, too. The Revolution was over, he told a friend, power was in the hands of central committees whose means of persuasion was the machine gun.

During his second long stay abroad—it lasted nearly a year and allowed him to spend enchanted weeks in Italy—he played with the idea of settling in Paris and supporting his little family as a taxi driver, like so many Russian expatriates. A cabby in France, he said, had more freedom than the president of a Soviet university. Nevertheless, he returned to Moscow, just in time to quash the sinister stories that were being spread about him. Thereafter no new work by him appeared. As he was incapable of compromise, he wrote in a letter, all he could do was retreat into himself. A book of his, dated 1936, is a reprint of previously issued writings, except for two plays. They had been printed earlier. *Sunset* was staged in Baku and Odessa (1927) and in Moscow (1928). Both there and, in 1966, in New York (off Broadway), it had a short run. The previous year, it was played in Budapest and Tel Aviv, and in 1966 also in Prague. *Maria,* his second play, was staged in Florence (1964), in Olomouc (Czechoslovakia, 1965), and in London (1967). Babel's last appearance in the Soviet press during his lifetime was with a wish for the New Year 1939. "With the passing of years," he wrote, "my admiration of the beauty and truth of those books has grown irrepressibly."

In certain influential circles his withdrawal into virtual silence was apt to be interpreted as disaffection. A Jew whose next of kin were expatriates, an author who had been adversely criticized by Bolshevik zealots, Babel was in a particularly vulnerable position. Some pressure to "produce" was brought to bear on him. He complained that he was tormented by demands to make public appearances and write "imbecile articles." Yet, oddly enough, with a ruthless purge of suspected dissenters raging around him, he was not seriously molested. In fact, in 1935 he was one of the Soviet delegates to the International Congress of Writers in Paris.

His circumstances were comfortable enough for him to be able to help his family abroad. His books sold well. And he had yet another source of income. Early in his career he had produced two movie scenarios, which were printed. The first, entitled *Benya Krik, A Cinema Tale,* belongs to the Odessa gangster series. Now he spent much of his time turning out scripts. He seems to have persuaded himself that such work, often done for the monetary return only, constituted no betrayal of his integrity as an artist. He had a flat in Moscow but often retired to a rented cottage in the country, his "village heaven." Later he acquired an admirable suburban villa. He traveled a good deal in the Ukraine, the Crimea, the Caucasus (on an assignment from *Pravda*), stayed in Kiev, made his way to Odessa for sea bathing, went to the races —not to play the horses but to feast his eyes on the beautiful creatures (he had caught the passion for horses from the Cossacks).

He was a man of a cheerful, resilient disposition, given to laughing "with his whole body," as a friend observed, and taking a childish delight in his own ready witticisms. "My *joie de vivre,*" he wrote to his sister in May, 1930, "never deserts me." As the terror mounted, his cheerfulness became a mask, concealing his state of mind from himself as well as from others. A housemate of his with whom he was on intimate terms jotted down in his diary in 1936: "Now I know that this man lives in fear, and not just occasionally." In writing to his mother and sister—his letters to his wife are not extant—Babel went out of his way to assure them that he was in no danger whatsoever. In fact, he painted his existence in idyllic colors. Thus, he is seen one autumn night seated at an open fire in his "splendid villa" and reading Sholom Aleichem's *Tevya, the Milkman* "in our highly original tongue," to use his own phrase. (His appreciation of Yiddish was in keeping with his loyalty to Odessa.)

The year 1939 found him "in fine working form." On May 10, he wrote to his mother that after finishing the script for a movie about Gorky he would turn to his "true work." He may have meant the project that he had conceived years earlier: a novel about rural collectivization. To judge by the two existing chapters (one printed posthumously in New York), the work, if completed, would have been a literary event. Babel was not given the opportunity to go on with that or with any other plan that he had had in mind. Five days after this letter went off he was arrested in Moscow and taken to the Lubyanka prison. His papers, which were seized by the police, vanished with him. The charge against him is not known. According to rumor, it was spying for Japan. Espionage in the interest of a foreign power almost invariably figured in the infamous Moscow trials. A certificate delivered to the family shortly after Stalin died gives March 17, 1941, as the date of Babel's death, but mentions neither its cause nor where it had occurred.

By way of rehabilitating a victim of Stalinist terror, the Military College of the Supreme Court of the U.S.S.R. stated in a notice dated December 23, 1954, that the sentence passed in the trial of I. E. Babel on January 24, 1940, had been revoked because of newly discovered circumstances, and the case terminated in the absence of a *corpus delicti*. Furthermore, a reprint of Babel's complete works appeared in 1957 under a Moscow imprint. A somewhat expanded edition was issued in 1966. Like the previous book, it was provided with an appreciative introduction.

Two different Yiddish versions of Babel's stories appeared as early as 1925, one printed in Kharkov, the other in Kiev. Translations into German, French, and Spanish came out during his lifetime. By now his stories are available in the major Western languages, as well as in modern Greek. His letters to his mother and sister were published in Italian and, under a New York imprint, in English.